KU-675-394

GARY NORTHFIELD

**WALKER
BOOKS**

For Arthur and Elsie, welcome to a
world of boneheads, nincompoops and
holibobs. And that's before you start
reading these books! Love Daddy.

Thank you as always to Lizzie and Chloé.
Sorry for all the extra grey hairs.

First published in Great Britain 2018 by Walker Books Ltd
87 Vauxhall Walk, London SE11 5HJ

2 4 6 8 10 9 7 5 3 1

© 2018 Gary Northfield

The right of Gary Northfield to be identified as author and illustrator
of this work has been asserted by him in accordance with the
Copyright, Designs and Patents Act 1988

This book has been typeset in Stempel Schneidler

Printed and bound in Great Britain by CPI Group (UK) Ltd, Croydon CR0 4YY

British Library Cataloguing in Publication Data:
a catalogue record for this book is available from the British Library

ISBN 978-1-4063-8096-5

www.walker.co.uk

CONTENTS

Julius wasn't like any other zebra and wasn't going to put up with this stranger's nonsense!

Exciting right?

❦ CHAPTER ONE ❦
ADVENTURE TIME!

"Oi!" cried Julius at the stranger. "You can't just go around chucking my friends through the air!"

WHO DO YOU THINK YOU ARE?!

"I told you!" laughed the muscle-bound man. "I am HERACLES, son of ZEUS, and I seek the champion named JULIUS ZEBRA and his friends for an exciting adventure!"

"Listen, Hairy Keith, son of Zoots," retorted Julius.

"Heracles!" corrected Heracles moodily.

"That's what I said," continued Julius. "I'm not looking for any more adventures!"

For one thing, my mum will kick me up the bottom!

Heracles seemed taken aback, and he bent over to have a good look at Julius. A big grin crept across his face and he gave a huge belly laugh.

"YOU?!" he exclaimed scornfully, and he took another close look at Julius, prodding him in his tummy and examining Julius's scrawny limbs.

YOU ARE NO CHAMPION!

POKE!

Heracles suddenly felt a kick to his shins and he spun round to find a crocodile looking at him crossly.

"You take that back, you big bully!" Lucia fumed. "Julius IS a champion, so you'd BETTER say sorry! I don't care WHO you are!"

Heracles laughed again. "Ha ha har!" he guffawed. "What strange, spirited creatures you are!" He gazed closely at the strange menagerie that stood before him. He grabbed Felix and held him in a headlock.

"And YOU, antelope, are YOU a great champion?"

Heracles let poor Felix drop to the ground as he paraded up and down in front of the animals, chuckling to himself.

"As you are no doubt aware," he boomed, "due to my vast legendary status, spanning the centuries and traversing all the known lands, I was tasked to complete twelve arduous labours."

"But it appears I was DECEIVED!" continued Heracles. "And one of my labours has since been UNDONE!" The demi-god waved his arms defiantly towards the skies. "My father and ruler of all the gods, ZEUS, demands that I finally complete this labour if am to take my place on Mount Olympus."

He turned directly to the animals. "I seek great champions to aid me on this quest, yet all I find are puny beasts CLAIMING to be the heroes of legend!"

He turned to face them and placed his giant hands on his hips in a dramatic pose. "So you leave me with little choice. You must PROVE your greatness to me!"

Cornelius had heard enough. "We don't have to prove ANYTHING to you!" squeaked the little warthog, wagging his trotter. "In fact, how do we know YOU are who you say you are, eh?"

Heracles strode towards a rocky outcrop where two gnus stood minding their own business. He crouched down and threw his two big arms around the boulder.

"If you have heard of me," Heracles declared, "then you know I am the STRONGEST BEING that has EVER lived!" Then, with a great roar, he began LIFTING the enormous rock in the air, his face going a deep red as the veins in his forehead looked ready to pop.

A ripple of applause rose from the entranced animals.

"Bravo!" cried Felix. "I'm TOTALLY convinced!"

Heracles performed a small bow, before hurling the boulder, with gnus in tow, towards the lake.

Julius was furious. "Can you PLEASE stop chucking animals about!!" he yelled.

Heracles laughed as he flexed his muscles. "Calm down, zebra. Have I not just proved that I am indeed the mightiest in all the lands?"

He placed a dusty hand on Julius's shoulder. "And now, you must prove who YOU are!"

"WE TOLD YOU!" interrupted Cornelius, still unimpressed. "We're not looking for any more adventures, so PUSH OFF!"

"Yeah!" agreed Julius. "Why should we listen to you anyway? What's in it for us?"

Heracles let out another of his deep guffaws. "What's in it for YOU?!" he laughed.

Those who help complete my final labour shall be granted IMMORTALITY!

"IMMORTALITY!?" parroted Julius. "We don't need your 'immortality', sunshine! Now sling yer hook!"

Julius turned to Cornelius. "What's 'immortality'?" he whispered.

"Immortality is where you get to live for ever and ever," replied Cornelius. "A bit like a god."

Julius raised an eyebrow. "So what, you don't die?"

"Not usually," said Cornelius.

Julius ran after Heracles, who had begun slowly striding away. "WAIT!" he called out. "We'll do it! We'll prove our greatness!"

Heracles turned round with a smug smile. "Excellent!" he proclaimed. "Already you show wisdom beyond your years!"

"What's Julius doing?!" cried Lucia, perplexed. "I thought we'd told that big buffoon to get lost?"

Cornelius held his head in his trotters. "Yes, but now that Heracles has promised us all immortality, Julius has had a change of heart!"

Brutus poked his nose into the conversation. "Immortality?" he sniffed. "What's that when it's at home?"

"Like I just told Julius, it's when you get to live for ever, like a god," said Cornelius, holding his snout. "Hey, I thought your mum told you to get rid of that stinky seaweed wig?!"

"Nothing comes between a zebra and his wig!" replied Brutus, brushing it gently with his hoof. "But forget all that – did you say we can be GODS?! NOW you're talking my language!"

As Cornelius buried his face once again in his trotters, a familiar figure approached the group.

"You're ALIVE!" cried Cornelius.

"Yes," growled Milus, brushing dust off his fur, "I'm alive." He gestured at Julius and Brutus. "Why are those IDIOTS talking to that lunatic?"

"We're all going to be GODS!" piped up Felix. "That big chap just promised us!"

Milus flopped backwards into the rough sand.

CHAPTER TWO
OLYMPIC GOLD MUDDLE

Hunched over, Julius placed his front hooves on the line scratched in the dirt. He bent his back legs, poised like two coiled springs ready to leap into action at a moment's notice.

Get ready to eat my dust!

"ON YOUR MARKS!" boomed Heracles, who stood to one side with his arm raised in the air. "GET SET..."

"GANGWAY!" cried Rufus as his long legs carried him through the mêlée and out clear in front.

"That's really not fair!" huffed Cornelius as he scuttled behind, desperately trying to keep up. "I've only got little legs!"

Suddenly the warthog felt something hard land on his head, and was shocked to find Brutus clomping over him like a stepping stone!

But, as Brutus went to leap off Lucia's head, a great tug on his tail yanked him out of the air and hard onto the dusty earth.

As the barging animals scrambled around the lake, Julius steeled himself with a deep breath and charged ahead with a great roar of determination. Julius was DESPERATE to prove to Heracles he was the legendary Champion of Rome worthy of his quest, and there was NO way he was going to let these idiots beat him!

Heracles sighed in solemn disappointment at the big tangle of arguing animals that lay at his feet.

"You cannot be the celebrated heroes whose names echo around the Roman Empire," he said, tutting and shaking his head.

"Well, apart from me, of course!" announced Julius brightly, dusting himself down. "I'm a proper legend, me!"

Heracles studied Julius quietly for a moment. "You are probably the MOST ridiculous!" he declared.

"Well, how rude!" protested Julius, frowning.

Not ONE of you are yet to prove to me that you are worthy of my new QUEST!

Julius let out a big gasp. "But I'm Julius Zebra!" he cried. "Champion of Rome, Saviour of Britannia, Liberator of Enslaved Beasts AND former Pharaoh of Egypt!"

Quest is my middle name!

Milus growled. "If your name gets any longer, donkey, I'm definitely going to have to eat you."

Unconvinced, Heracles strode to the edge of the lake. "Follow me!" he declared.

Thrusting his hands into the water, he pulled out a large, flat, smooth stone. Standing at the edge with his back to the lake, Heracles swung the heavy stone in his outstretched hand across his chest. He then quickly and dramatically spun round three times, before loosing the stone across the entire expanse of water.

Heracles turned to Julius and the others. "You lot next!" he commanded. "Hit that tree and I'll know for a FACT that you're worthy of helping me complete my labour!"

"That's ridiculous!" blurted Felix. "That's MILES away! We'll NEVER hit it from here!"

"This just gets stupider and stupider!" huffed Brutus, folding his arms in indignation.

"If you do not hit it, then you will have failed and I, in turn, will also have failed," said Heracles. "You will NOT be the bold adventurers that I have been seeking."

Julius stepped forward and walked to the water's edge. "Watch THIS!" he said.

After a quick scrabble around in the musky water, Julius pulled out a suitable stone.

I'll show you who's the legend around here!

Julius stood with his back to the lake and held out the stone in front of him, just like Heracles had done.

Then, desperately trying to remember the next moves, he spun his arms like windmills and threw himself into full-body rotation, twirling round and round, his arms outstretched like a spinning top. With a great gurgling grunt, he launched the stone high into the air.

Backwards.

The whole lakeside erupted into laughter.

"Nice work, legend!" snickered Milus.

Cornelius ran up to his friend and patted him on the back. "Don't listen to them, Julius," he said. "I'd like to see them get it right the first time! Why don't you go next, Felix?"

"NO WAY!" spluttered the antelope, clutching a new rock he'd just found. "I collect rocks, not chuck them away!!"

Suddenly, Rufus strode up carrying Julius's stone. "Make way!" he said confidently. "I'll show you how it's done!"

Rufus held the pose for about ten seconds before everyone started to get restless.

"Throw it, then!" laughed Brutus. "I thought you said you saw it on a jug?"

Rufus's face grew bright red with embarrassment and he started sweating. "Yeah, well, they didn't show the next step."

"But you just watched Heracles!" Lucia reasoned. "Just copy him!"

Heracles buried his face in the palms of his hands. "We are doomed," he moaned. "Totally lost..."

"Give me that stone," growled Milus, snatching it from Rufus. The straggly-maned lion flipped the discus-shaped stone into the air and deftly caught it behind his back with his other paw.

Milus held up his empty paw to shield the sun from his eyes in order to get a clear look at the tree. The lion then took up the pose demonstrated by Heracles, held it for two seconds, then spun round quickly three times, releasing the stone long and fast towards the tree.

There's a lot more to it than staring at crockery!

Heracles gave the lion a big pat on the back and ruffled his mane. "Yes, lion, that was INDEED impressive," he conceded. "A heroic effort!"

Unhappy at having his mane ruffled, Milus went to lunge at the burly Greek, but Rufus and Lucia held him back.

"Careful, Milus!" warned Cornelius. "The Heracles of legend defeated many lions!"

But Milus was having none of it. "If he's so tough and legendary," he sneered, "why is he so keen to recruit us idiots?"

Heracles towered above Milus, his imposing size casting a great shadow over the tatty lion. "And who says I'm going to recruit you?" he snapped. "NONE of you have yet completed my tasks!"

He leant into Milus's face. "You came close, lion, but you DIDN'T HIT IT!"

Suddenly Cornelius splashed into the water and found himself a big flat stone. "Let's put a stop to this nonsense, once and for all!" he squeaked.

Heracles burst into deep, rumbling laughter. "And I suppose YOU will hit it, little piglet?"

Ignoring the taunt, Cornelius took up position on the lakeside facing the tree. But this time, Cornelius eschewed the familiar pose as displayed by Heracles and Roman jugs and adopted his own unique stance.

Holding the stone tight under his belly, Cornelius skimmed it across the lake and it skipped majestically across the surface of the water all the way to the faraway tree, clattering into it with a faint clonk.

Heracles lifted Cornelius up high and everyone
cheered again.

"You'll need brains as well as brawn where you'll
be going!" laughed Heracles.

But, while everyone was caught up in the
celebrations, Julius spotted his brother splashing
about by the water's edge.

"Brutus, what are you doing?" asked Julius.

"I haven't had MY go!" shouted Brutus as he
swished his arms around. "I want to be immortal too!"

He held up a massive rock.

"This'll do!" he declared. "WATCH ME,
EVERYBODY! WATCH ME!"

Brutus stood at the edge of the lake and held up his extremely heavy rock.

Cornelius tried to stop him. "Brutus!" he shouted. "That's completely the wrong-shaped rock!"

But it was no use. Sticking his tongue out in concentration, Brutus began twirling very quickly, his rock held outstretched in his hooves.

With a deep, grunting "OOOFF!!" Brutus FLUNG his boulder high into the air and over the lake, but its great size and weight meant it didn't stay airborne for long. With a loud PLOP, the rock plunged into the water.

And with a huge ROAR, a giant hippo leapt from the lake clutching her head in pain.

"Oh, good work, Brutus!" sighed Julius.

"LEG IT!" cried Brutus as everybody made a mad dash away from the angry hippo.

"NOW I'm impressed!" laughed Heracles. "You're all pretty good at running away and there'll be PLENTY of that on my adventure!"

❦CHAPTER THREE❧
BEAST QUEST

The journey to the port of Leptis Magna, where Heracles's ship was anchored, was a few hours away. Thankfully, Heracles had his own horses and cart for them all to ride on.

As Heracles drove them towards the port, there were grumblings of disquiet among the animals.

Cornelius shuffled up next to Julius to talk to him without being overheard. "Julius!" he whispered. "I'm really not sure why on earth we're doing this."

"To gain immortality!" replied Julius just as quietly. "You heard the man."

"Yes, I know, but why us?"

"Because we're CHAMPIONS!"

"Shh!" said a panicked Cornelius, waving his trotter. "Not so loud!"

"Cornelius wants to know why we're going on an exciting adventure!" whispered Julius.

"I thought we were all going to be immortals?" replied Felix.

"That's what I told him!" said Julius.

"Don't you want to be immortal, Cornelius?" asked Felix, all concerned. "It'll be a brilliant laugh! Imagine living for ever; I'd be able to collect every rock ever invented!"

"Imagine all the birthdays!" said Lucia, clapping.

"And all that cake!" added Felix.

Everyone nodded in approval.

"And when people ask you how old you are," said Julius, getting excited, "you could say something like, 'I am one million, two thousand, three hundred and thirty-two'!"

Cornelius waved everybody into a huddle, keeping one eye on Heracles, who was busy driving the cart. "It's not that bit I'm unsure about," he whispered.

Something's not right.

"What concerns me is why he is asking US to do this task, as opposed to doing it himself."

"What do you mean?" asked a confused Julius.

"Well," said Cornelius, "he keeps going on about us helping him complete his 'unfinished labour'!"

"Yeah, so?" Julius shrugged. "He just needs a little assistance. No biggie!"

"But that's my point!" said Cornelius sternly. "It IS a biggie." He glanced around again at Heracles, who was happily whistling to himself unawares.

"I know all about his 'legendary' labours and they were tasked to Heracles as a PUNISHMENT and only Heracles himself should complete them."

"If Zeus finds out he's got us idiots to help him," whispered Cornelius, "he might not look too favourably on Heracles or us, and who knows what sort of punishments he might dish out?"

"Oh, stop worrying!" pleaded Julius. "Heracles is a proper LEGEND, so he's not going to start being all devious, is he?"

"You think?" replied Cornelius, not at all convinced. "Do we even know what this so-called quest is? Half of his original labours involved wrestling MONSTERS!"

"I agree with Cornelius," growled Milus. "I wouldn't trust that man as far as I could throw him."

"Well, he obviously trusts you!" sniggered Brutus. "He threw you for MILES!"

Heracles turned round to see what the fuss was. "What ails thee?" he cried, surveying the nervous-looking animals. "Have you seen ghosts?"

Cornelius was about to reply, but Julius quickly butted in. "Er, we were just wondering," he said. "Do we have to wrestle any monsters on this quest?"

Heracles burst out laughing. "No, there'll be no monsters," he snickered. "You're going to help me find an APPLE!"

"An APPLE!?" blurted Julius. "Is that it?!"

Julius turned to everyone in the cart. "See!" he said, smiling. "Easy-peasy!"

"Yes, but not just ANY apple!" laughed Heracles.

"A GOLDEN APPLE?!" everyone cried in shock.

"Where'd we find one of THOSE?" exclaimed Felix.

"This is why I require your help!" replied Heracles. "My original apple was deemed too sacred by my meddling sister, Athene, and she returned it to the far off land from whence it came." Heracles looked off into the distance as he remembered his past labour. "It was a difficult task to acquire such a prized artefact, so I was reluctant to retrace my steps. But not two weeks ago, I was chatting to a well-travelled adventurer, who had heard tell of a golden apple slipping from a warrior's pocket as he picked his way through a Labyrinth."

Did you say, "Labyrinth"?!

"Yes, I did!" replied Heracles. "A HUGE maze, far too big for one man to search, so that's where you chaps come in!"

Heracles suddenly pulled on the reins and halted the horses. He looked gravely at the animals. "But you must promise me one thing," he said, and he waved them all to lean closer. "You must not tell a soul of our quest!" he whispered.

"Why not?" asked Cornelius suspiciously.

"I don't want my interfering sister finding out about it and betraying me to Zeus ... I mean spoiling my surprise," replied Heracles. "Zeus loves surprises, so I want to gift him the apple myself!"

"Ooh, I love surprises!" Lucia clapped.

"Yes, and so does Zeus," said Heracles. "So keep it under your hats. NO ONE must know what we're up to!" With a snap of the reins, the horses began pulling the cart once again.

See! Nothing to worry about at all!

Ruffle!

"Yeah," harrumphed Cornelius. "Apart from the fact labyrinths are KNOWN to have monsters in them AND we have to keep quiet, there's nothing to worry about AT ALL!"

"Heracles PLAINLY said there'll be no monsters, so please stop worrying!" said Julius. "This is our best chance at being proper IMMORTAL HEROES, just like Heracles! We'll be more famous than EVER! People will sing songs about us!"

"Will we have our pictures on the side of jugs?" asked Felix excitedly.

"Almost certainly!" replied Julius.

"Oh wow!" replied Felix. "I've always wanted to have my face on a jug!"

Hush, my friends! We have reached our port.

Adventure awaits!

CHAPTER FOUR
LOYALTY CAD

Before they set off, Heracles gathered everyone together.

"My friends, we are about to embark on an exciting adventure. As with all adventures, I must warn you, we may encounter great peril along the way..."

"Having searched high and low throughout many lands," continued Heracles, "I have found YOU, heroes of the Roman Empire, more than worthy of the task assigned by Zeus himself and any dangers we may encounter!" He raised a fist to his chest and thumped it. "I, Heracles, son of Zeus, ask you, my new-found adventurers, to pledge your loyalty to me and the task bestowed upon us."

"We do!" cried Julius enthusiastically.

"We do?" asked Cornelius. "No one said anything about pledges!" he complained.

"If you are with me," said Heracles, "then raise your fist to your chest and swear!"

"I don't have a fist," said Brutus. "Can we use hooves?"

"Yes, of course."

"And claws?" asked Lucia.

"Yes, yes," said Heracles impatiently, "hooves, claws, trotters, whatever you have."

"And if you don't want to swear?" growled Milus.

"Then you are free to leave. Although, you may find it a long walk home."

"Come on, Milus!" urged Julius. "Going on an adventure wouldn't be the same without your cheery face!"

"Oh, yeah," muttered Felix, "you can't beat having a lion sat next to you, day in, day out, to keep you on your trotters!"

Milus looked at Felix for a moment, then turned to Julius. "All right, I'll come," he said. "At the very least, I'll know I'll never go hungry." He grinned at Felix.

Can we also pledge not to eat each other?

Heracles was getting impatient. "So, are we in agreement?" Everyone nodded. "Then put your fist – sorry, hoof, claw, trotter, paw – to your chest and swear your loyalty!"

We swear our loyalty!

Cornelius raised his trotter and gave a little cough.

"Yes, warthog," said Heracles, "you have a question?"

"Thank you," squealed Cornelius. "Now we've pledged ourselves to you and to Zeus's task, what happens if we DON'T complete it? Does that mean we'll be in trouble with Zeus?"

"Well," said Heracles, looking very serious for a moment. "If we DON'T find the golden apple then Zeus will banish us to Hades!" He then clapped his hands enthusiastically. "So let's make sure that doesn't happen, eh?" And he bounded gleefully to the ropes mooring the ship to the jetty and untied them.

Julius shrugged. "I'm sure it's nothing to worry about!"

"NOTHING TO WORRY ABOUT!" squealed

Cornelius. "You do know what HADES is, right?"

Julius looked blank for a moment. "That strange place north of Hadrian's Wall?"

Cornelius nearly exploded. "NO, JULIUS! IT'S LITERALLY IN THE PITS OF HELL! WHERE YOU GO WHEN YOU'RE DEAD!"

"Am I surrounded by NINCOMPOOPS?" screamed Cornelius.

"Do you really want me to answer that?" replied Milus drily.

Julius tried to calm his little friend down. "Relax, Cornelius, you're making a bit of a scene!"

"Of COURSE I'm making a scene!" rasped

Cornelius. "If we don't find this stupid apple, we get sent to HELL!"

"If it's that bad," interjected Brutus, trying his best to help, "why don't we tell Heracles we don't want to do the quest after all?"

"Because you just swore loyalty to my cause," interrupted Heracles, who had been standing calmly watching them squabble.

Cornelius swung round to face the Greek demigod. "You rotter!" he protested. "Why didn't you tell us about Hades before we swore loyalty?"

"Do not panic, little warthog," said Heracles, smiling. "Few people get banished to Hades, and some of them have even been rescued!"

"Only some?" replied Cornelius.

"Now come on!" he implored. "Let's sail this ship out to sea!" Straining with all his might, he hauled up the anchor and directed Rufus and Lucia to hoist the sail. With Milus and Felix at the tiller, the ship finally sailed slowly out from the harbour into the open sea.

Heracles stood dramatically at the bows, one hand on his hip, the other shielding his eyes from the sun.

"Head north east!" he declared.

We sail for CRETE!

He jumped back onto the deck. "We'll be there in three days, where this task will be swiftly accomplished!"

He rubbed Cornelius's hairy head. "So put to bed any notions of failure!"

"Brilliant," huffed Cornelius, brushing his wiry hair

back into place. "Crete. This trip keeps getting better and better. That's LITERALLY where they keep a monster in a labyrinth."

"Come on, Cornelius," said Julius. "You really need to start trusting the guy. If Heracles says there'll be no monsters, then there'll be NO monsters!"

"Old Heracles here is supposed to be a legend," retorted Cornelius, poking his trotter towards their new companion. "But there he stands as bold as brass!"

"Look," said Julius, growing slightly weary of Cornelius's moaning. "If we DO find any monsters, I completely promise to tackle them first. You won't have to go anywhere near them."

Suddenly, out of the corner of his eye, Cornelius spotted something moving beside Julius's hoof.

"Look out, Julius!" he cried. "Mind you don't step on that crab!"

Cornelius picked up the bewildered crab and plopped it safely over the side. "So much for my brave guardian!"

A flustered Julius shrugged his shoulders as if nothing had happened. "Yeah, well," he mumbled, "crabs are different."

CHAPTER FIVE
HEAVY METAL

The small merchant ship sailed gently on the clear, calm surface of the beautiful deep blue Mediterranean Sea. Julius and Cornelius stood on deck looking out towards the horizon as a gentle breeze cooled their faces.

Well, this makes a change from throwing up our breakfast or being smashed onto rocks!

Julius patted his old chum on the shoulder. "I know you're not keen on this quest, Cornelius, but I have a good feeling about this adventure!"

"How so?" asked Cornelius doubtfully.

"Well, I feel we're more in control of our own destiny, don't you?"

"Not really." Cornelius shrugged despondently.

"Oh, come on!" protested Julius. "On all our other adventures we were THRUST into danger! Kidnapped by Romans then thrown into the Colosseum; packed off to Britannia by Emperor Hadrian; then, to top it all off, shipwrecked in Egypt!"

Julius gazed out again across the calm sea. "I think this adventure is going to be the making of us. Because, this time, WE'RE in charge!"

Cornelius let out a less than convinced sigh and looked up to see squawking seagulls swirling above their ship.

Cornelius didn't finish his sentence. Instead he stood on tiptoe and strained his eyes, trying to get a better look at the gulls.

"Wait, what's that thing up there with the seagulls?"

Julius looked up too. "What? That large round thing? How odd. Is it me, or is it actually getting bigger?"

Cornelius grabbed Julius by the arm and dragged him away from the ship's bows.

"IT IS! AND IT'S COMING TOWARDS US!" he screamed. "RUN, JULIUS!!!"

"WHAT WAS THAT???" screamed Julius as he dangled helplessly over the side of the ship. Cornelius lay flat on the deck, face down and eyes shut.

"THE SKY'S FALLING ON OUR HEADS!" squealed the little warthog. "WE'RE DOOMED! DOOMED!!"

Suddenly, another huge object flew in front of the sun, casting a great shadow over the ship.

"LOOK OUT!" cried Julius, as he scrambled back on board. "HERE COMES ANOTHER ONE!!"

As the ship bobbed and swayed from the shock waves, Rufus craned his long neck and peered in the direction of the flying boulders.

"FLIPPIN' 'ECK!" he exclaimed, giving his disbelieving eyeballs a good rub. "It's not the sky falling in! Look!" And he pointed towards a looming shape on the horizon.

"IT'S A MASSIVE BLOKE AND HE'S CHUCKING ROCKS AT US!!"

"THE NEXT BOULDER WILL HIT US FOR CERTAIN!" cried Felix, as he desperately clung on to the mast. "WE HAVE TO DO SOMETHING!"

"DID YOU SAY A GIANT MAN?" called out Heracles to Rufus.

"YES!" replied Rufus. "And judging by the way the sun glints off him, I'd say he's made of METAL!"

"WHAT?" exclaimed Julius. "You KNOW who he is?!"

"Yes," replied Heracles. "He is the guardian of

Crete, protecting the island from pirates and invaders. I had hoped to escape his notice!"

"Ooh!" gasped Lucia. "Are we pirates now? How exciting!"

"BUT HOW CAN WE STOP A BIG METAL STATUE?!" yelled Julius, barely able to stand as he pulled himself back over the side.

Cornelius suddenly lifted his head up from his trotters.

Metal statue, you say?

The little warthog leapt to his feet and scuttled over to the bow to see for himself. "Then we must get him WET!" he declared.

"WET?!" spluttered Julius. "WHAT ARE YOU BABBLING ABOUT?"

"He's a big metal man. If we get him wet, he'll rust up and stop moving."

Ergo, he'll stop throwing rocks at us!

Julius looked perplexed. "But how are we going to get him wet? It's not like we have magic powers to make it rain or anything."

Everyone turned to stare at Julius.

"What?" he asked angrily. "Why are you all looking at me?"

"Well, you know," piped up Felix. "ONE of us has powers to make it rain..."

DON'T BE RIDICULOUS!!!

Julius stormed off to the stern of the ship. "HOW MANY TIMES?!" he raged. "I DON'T HAVE MAGIC POWERS!!"

Lucia followed the sulking zebra. "Come on, Julius," she coaxed. "What harm could it do?"

Julius sniffed and gazed out to sea, pretending to ignore her.

"Imagine if it did work?" she continued. "You'd be a hero!" She patted him on the back. "And if it didn't? Well, at least you'd have tried."

Lucia stared at the others. "You wouldn't think Julius was an idiot if it didn't work, would you?"

Heracles came over and put his arm round Julius. "Do this and it will be your first step towards greatness!"

Julius slowly turned round. "Are you sure?" he whispered bashfully.

"YES!" bellowed Heracles confidently. "There are not many that walk the earth that can stop Talos, but I sense you are one of them!"

Julius looked at his friends. "And are you sure you won't think I'm an idiot?"

"Of course not!" they all cried.

"GREAT!" he exclaimed, suddenly rejuvenated, and clapping his hooves.

Rufus pointed to a large silhouette standing next to what looked like a harbour. "Just on that fellow there, please!"

"Righto!" agreed Julius, and immediately went into an impressive trance.

Everyone eagerly watched the heavens to see if anything stirred.

Nothing did.

Julius dropped his arms to his sides and flopped to the deck in despair. "I knew it," he groaned. "I TOLD you I didn't have magical powers."

But as his friends went over to console him, Cornelius looked up to see another dark shadow in the sky. "Look out!" he wailed. "Another boulder!"

Expecting the worse, everyone dived for cover.

But no boulder came.

Cornelius looked up again at the sky only to see dark grey clouds forming over the nearby island.

Then came a crack of thunder, and the heavens opened with a torrential downpour.

In the distance, a great hollow creaking noise reverberated through the air.

"That noise, it's Talos!" cried Rufus. "I think he's seizing up!"

On the horizon, the giant metal colossus swayed awkwardly as the rain began rusting up his joints.

"That's amazing!" gasped Julius. "Look how he's waving his arms around in despair!"

"Ha ha!" laughed Cornelius. "He's really struggling." But then the warthog took a closer look. "Wait, he's not struggling!" he squealed. "He's throwing another boulder! LOOK OUT!!"

"So much for him seizing up!" cried Julius as he grabbed on to a broken piece of the ship.

Rufus bobbed next to him, holding on to the wooden fragment for dear life. "Actually," he said, peering towards the colossus, "I think he's properly seized up now! Nice work!"

"Oh yeah, brilliant," spluttered Julius. "Well done me."

Julius pushed off from the wreckage with his back legs. "I'm not waiting to find out how angry a dolphin can get. Come on!" And off he splashed, heading towards the harbour.

But, as everyone started to swim after Julius, Cornelius spotted Heracles paddling off in the opposite direction.

"JULIUS!" cried out Cornelius. "HERACLES IS GOING THE WRONG WAY!"

Julius looked round to see Heracles disappearing off into the distance.

Heracles called out something and gave them a big wave.

"SPEAK UP!" shouted Julius. "I CAN'T HEAR YOU!"

"I think he said something about looking elsewhere for the apple," said Cornelius, straining to hear Heracles. "WHERE SHALL WE MEET YOU AGAIN?" he yelled. "SHALL WE WAIT FOR YOU IN CRETE?"

Heracles gave a big thumbs up, then held up two fingers.

"IN TWO DAYS?" cried Julius, trying to work out what the demi-god was saying.

Heracles shook his head.

"TWO WEEKS, THEN?" guessed Cornelius.

Heracles held his thumb aloft again, then turned and carried on swimming until soon he was just a tiny dot.

"Well, that's not weird," said Julius.

It's almost like Talos knew that idiot was on our boat.

Don'tchathink?

"What have I been trying to tell you?" replied Cornelius.

Julius glanced nervously at Cornelius, then, without any further comment, continued swimming towards the shore.

❧ CHAPTER SIX ❧
SPA-RRING PARTNER

As Julius paddled to shore, he was amazed at
how jolly and friendly the Cretan port seemed.
Children splashed about in the water, while their
parents relaxed in the hot sun. On the promenade,
pretty tavernas and restaurants were dotted among
the fishermen's huts. Melodic sounds of stringed
instruments intertwined with the smell of food
wafting from open doors.

"I could get used to this!" marvelled Julius.

Lucia tugged at his arm. "Hey, Julius, check out
these guys over here! What fun!"

"Hold on a second!" exclaimed Julius. "Is that our old friend PLINY?!"

The little mouse leading the aqua aerobics fell backwards into the water in shock. "DEBRA!!!" he screamed. "Who gave your ugly mug permission to be on this island?" He leapt out of the sea and gave Julius a big hug around the neck.

"I thought you were heading back to Rome to try out your new fighting skills?" said Cornelius as he embraced his old friend.

"That was the plan!" squealed Pliny, and he dropped into the surf and ran up to Felix who was scouring the beach for rocks.

"Oh, hello, Pliny!" said Felix innocently.

"Wotcha, bonehead!" said Pliny, jumping onto the unsuspecting antelope's head, and grabbing his horns.

SPLOSH!

Brushing the sand off his paws, Pliny sauntered back up the beach to a round of applause from his old friends. "I fell in love with Crete's balmy climate and delicious grub, so I ended up staying here, learning a few more nifty moves while I was at it!" He cracked his tiny knuckles. "That's what is known as a Cretan Curler!"

Pliny pointed to a smart little building further along the beach. "And now I've even got my very own health spa for retired gladiators!"

"YOUR OWN HEALTH SPA!" exclaimed Julius. "Amazing! What's a health spa?"

Pliny jumped back towards the old folk in the sea and started doing star jumps, which they duly copied. "It's a place that helps ya keep fit and healthy in your old age! Hup, one! Hup, two!"

Curiosity got the better of Cornelius. "But don't you need money to open a new business?" he asked.

"Ha ha ha!" laughed Pliny. "NOTHING gets past wise old Cornelius!"

Pliny waved his arms. "After our shenanigans in Egypt, I still had a couple of them gold armbands. So, after a bit of moseying around the Med, I cashed them in, pitched up here and Bob's yer uncle!"

Pliny skipped about, full of excitement to be reunited with his old pals. "Who'd have guessed I'd be so happy to see your ugly mugs!"

"So I take it old Emperor Hadrian has forgiven you, then?"

"Forgiven me for what?" asked Julius, slightly confused.

"For turning down his job offer. You proper upset him back in Egypt."

"They ARE?!" yelped Julius, quickly ducking under the water. After a couple of seconds, he came up for air. "I can't stay under there all day!" he spluttered. "YOU HAVE TO HIDE US, PLINY!!"

Pliny gave a big tut. "You GUYS!" he squeaked, scanning the beach for Romans. "What are you EVEN doing here in the FIRST place?"

"We're on a SECRET MISSION!" declared Lucia. "And I think we're going to need your help with disguises!" She rubbed her claws with glee at the prospect of exciting subterfuge.

"Ooh!" cried Pliny, backflipping off Milus's head into the soft sand. "A secret mission, you say!" He started darting about, karate-chopping the air, somersaulting backwards and kicking little rocks into the sea as if they were dangerous foes. "I could do with a bit of a break from all this relaxing. Where are you headed?"

"The labyrinth!" announced Julius proudly.

THE LABYRINTH?!

ARE YOU BONKERS?!!

"We're just going to pick up a golden apple!" laughed Brutus, flicking back his seaweed wig. "Easy-peasy!"

"Golden apple?" exclaimed Pliny. "There's no golden apple in the labyrinth, only a nasty Minotaur!"

"Minotaur?" echoed Julius.

"Yeah, Minotaur!" replied Pliny. "Half man, half bull. Proper big monster – you don't stand a chance!"

Pliny started back to his aerobic class, "So, you can count me out."

Julius ran after him. "But please, Pliny," he pleaded. "If we don't find this apple, we're in BIG trouble. We need all the help we can get!"

Pliny looked Julius straight in the eye. "No one in their right mind goes to that poo-hole. NO ONE!"

"But, Julius has magic powers!" cried Lucia. "He stopped that big metal giant with a rain cloud only this morning!"

Pliny burst out laughing. "Julius didn't stop old Talos with his magic powers," he scoffed. "Crete ALWAYS has sudden rain bursts!" He pointed to the giant silhouette in the distance. "That metal monster is FOREVER rusting up!"

"Then help us!" implored Julius. "You must know this place so well."

Come on, it'll be like old times!

Oi!

Pliny paused for a moment to ponder what madness he would be letting himself in for. "Gah!" he cried. "OK, I'm in, but we HAVE to sort you out some disguises, or the Romans will get you before any monster can."

The little mouse dashed towards his spa.

"This way!" he ordered, and held open a door.

As they all rushed to follow him, Julius realized someone was missing. "Where's Felix?" he asked.

"Where do you think?" growled Milus as he went inside.

Julius looked back to the beach to see the antelope hunched over, rifling through the pebbles and rocks.

"HURRY, FELIX!" he shouted.

"Just get inside!" barked Julius, before casting a final nervous glance around the beach to make sure no Roman soldiers were watching them.

Inside, they found themselves in a hot and steamy corridor. The sound of swishing water and slapping, mixed with laughter and the odd grunt and groan, reverberated through the spa. An elderly gentleman wrapped in a wet towel squeezed past them and gave them all a polite nod.

"This place is weird!" muttered Julius.

Pliny ushered them into a small room.

"Just wait in here," he ordered, and dashed off down the corridor.

"That is proper amazing!" gasped Brutus, peering through his seaweed locks. "What a strange and wondrous land Crete is!"

"It's a hermit crab," said Cornelius with a deflated huff.

"Ooh!" said Brutus, eyeing up the crab. "A helmet crab!"

"So it's not a rock with little legs, then?" sighed Felix, poking his new find.

"No," replied Cornelius, "it's a little crab that lives in a shell."

Pliny re-entered the room carrying a tower of clothes and weapons.

"We need to make tracks sharpish!" he gasped, dropping the bundle on the floor. "Your arrival has already caused a bit of a stir, so we'd better hoof it before the local legion gets wind!"

"Where did you find this stuff?" asked Julius, admiring his long spear.

"Let's just say there's a group in the steam bath who are going to be VERY upset when they go to get dressed in five minutes," replied Pliny with a smirk.

As they sneaked out of the side door and onto the main road, Pliny turned to Julius and handed him a strange object.

CHAPTER SEVEN
AMAZEBALLS

Julius hated exercise and, as he quickly discovered, he particularly hated trudging up steep hills made of dry crumbly gravel that gave way under his hooves. The garments he was wearing didn't help either.

Whose idea was it to go trekking up hills in heavy armour?

"You won't be moaning about wearing armour when you face that 'orrible Minotaur!" squeaked Pliny, who was skipping out ahead. "Come on, not far now! Just over this ridge!"

"Some palace!" gasped Julius, leaning on his spear in exhaustion. "It's in ruins!"

"Yeah," replied Pliny, skipping towards the rubble, "a big earthquake saw to that!"

Come on! The labyrinth is hidden underneath!

Straightening up, Julius tramped towards the remains of the palace, followed wearily by the others.

"I can't say I like the look of this place!" worried Cornelius, trying his best to keep up in his heavy, oversized armour.

"Look," reasoned Julius, "if this place is so old and decrepit, there's no WAY there's still a Minotaur down there!"

"I hope you're right," sighed the little warthog gloomily.

"Come on!" said Julius enthusiastically. "Let's grab that golden apple, head back to one of those nice tavernas and have ourselves a little holibob while we wait for Heracles to come back."

"You're forgetting the whole of the Roman army is looking for us," huffed Cornelius. "Hanging out in tavernas isn't exactly an option!"

Everyone caught up with Pliny, who was standing impatiently at the foot of the palace ruins.

I'm pretty sure this is the entrance!

The old granite door was slightly ajar so Julius tiptoed up to the crack to see if he could peer inside. He immediately recoiled, retching. "PEEYOOO!" he cried, desperately trying to catch his breath. "This place flippin' STINKS!"

Felix suddenly became really excited as he spotted
a glinting object on the ground by the door.

"Woohoo!" he exclaimed. "I bagsy the big sword!"

But as he picked it up, everyone screamed and
started running away.

"SKELLYBOB!" yelled Julius, hiding behind a big
boulder.

Confused, Felix went to grab the handle of the
sword, only to put his hoof on the bony remains.

Screaming, Felix ran to the big boulder behind which everyone was now hiding. "Thanks for leaving me with the skellybob hand, ya rotters!" he huffed.

With a growl, Milus stood up, pulled his helmet firmly down, raised his shield and marched towards the entrance. "This is ridiculous!" he muttered under his breath. He put his shoulder against the heavy granite door and pushed with all his might.

Julius and the others joined Milus and they all heaved against the dusty slab. Slowly they gathered momentum until finally, after one big SHOVE, the giant door scraped inwards to reveal a long, gloomy, STINKY passageway.

"That is ROTTEN!" said Rufus, holding his nose. "It makes your seaweed wig seem like a bunch of fragrant flowers, Brutus!"

As the rest of them stumbled backwards to catch a breath of fresh air, Julius leant further in, squinting at the passageway floor. "Can anyone see a golden apple? Please tell me it's right here by the door!"

Everyone inched in gingerly, gazes scouring the floor.

"It's no good," said Lucia after a moment. "I can't see a thing!" She turned round. "We need your lamp, Felix!"

But Felix was nowhere to be seen.

"FELIX?!" called out Lucia. "Where ARE you?"

A timid voice piped up from behind the big boulder. "I ain't coming over there!"

"Oh, come on!" shouted Julius. "Stop being a baby!"

"I don't go nowhere near SKELLYBOBS," Felix rasped. "So I'll see you when you get back!"

Cornelius trotted back to the boulder. "You know, Felix, old bones are sometimes called fossils, and fossils are in fact ROCKS!"

"Absolutely!" replied Cornelius. "Imagine how amazing your collection will look after this adventure. You'll be the envy of ALL rock collectors!"

There was a long pause, before a familiar pair of horns appeared from behind the boulder and Felix bounded over to the smelly doorway. "Well, why didn't you SAY?" From his knapsack he pulled out his little oil lamp, metal striker and pocket flint. He struck the flint and with the spark lit the lamp's wick.

As they nervously ventured inside, Pliny suddenly stopped Julius. "WAIT!" he cried. "Don't forget your string!"

Julius pulled out the ball from his tunic.

"Brilliant!" said Julius, holding the string firmly. "What do I do with it?"

"Oh … er … I don't know that bit," spluttered Pliny. "Chuck it at the Minotaur, probably!"

"Gotcha!" replied Julius confidently. "Then let's go find us an apple. And no Minotaur had better get in our way!"

But, just as they were about to head further inside, Cornelius held up his trotter to stop them. "Look!" he squealed and pointed at one of the skellybobs lining the corridor. "What's that he's holding in his hand?"

Cornelius grabbed it excitedly and held it up to have a good look. "I think it's a scroll!"

"Does it tell us to go home?" asked a nervous Brutus. "Cause I'm thinking that's a good idea."

Cornelius unrolled the old piece of parchment and his eyes lit up. "I can't believe it!" he gasped. "What amazing luck!"

Cornelius handed the map to Julius. "Here you go, Julius," he said. "You wanted to go first, remember?"

"I did?" gulped Julius.

"Yes," said Cornelius. "You promised you'd be the first to tackle any monsters we found."

Julius nervously took the map. "Oh yeah," he stuttered, "so I did." He looked at the map for a while, tapping his chin. "Right," he said confidently, "we need to go through this door."

"We've DONE that, donkey!" growled Milus pointing at the map. "Just lead the way!"

"This is RIDICULOUS!" huffed Julius. "We've been walking for HOURS!"

Cornelius examined a bundle of bones sat in the corner. "Yes, I'm sure we've passed here before…"

I definitely recognize that face!

Milus stormed up to Julius and snatched the map out of his hooves. "How is it we're lost, when you have an actual MAP?"

"Yeah, all right, grumpy guts!" Julius blustered. "Map-reading was never one of my strong points."

Milus glowered at the zebra. "Do you even HAVE a strong point?"

Milus flapped the map out flat in front of his nose and examined it carefully, then looked at the walls and passageways around them.

Julius prodded the map with his hoof. "I've been trying to get us to this bit at the bottom here with the strange writing and big arrow."

Milus looked closely at the writing.

"I don't know what the words mean," continued Julius. "They're probably in really old Greek, but I bet it says something really important, like 'Here be treasure!'"

Milus looked again closely at the writing and twisted the map around one hundred and eighty degrees. He then crushed the map in one paw and slapped his forehead with the other.

"You've had the map upside down the whole time!" Milus raged.

"How dare you! No I haven't!" protested Julius indignantly, snatching the crumpled map back. Smoothing it out, he looked at it again and then at their surroundings. "Wait. How can you tell?"

Milus stabbed the map with a claw. "Because these *strange* words you've been struggling with are in fact upside-down words. Those *strange* words do in fact say: 'This way up'."

Snarling, Milus snatched back the map and stalked to the front alongside Felix. "Everybody follow me!"

As they weaved their way through the wretched, vile-smelling passageways, Milus spotted a faint glow ahead. He held up his arm. "I think we've found him," he growled.

Julius shuffled his way to the front, holding out his ball of string. "Good work, Milus!" he declared. "I'll take over from here!"

I'll bonk him on the head with this string, grab the apple and we'll be off!

"Careful, Debra!" whispered Pliny. "They reckon the Minotaur is a big, nasty brute." The little mouse picked up a small rock and threw it at one of the skulls that littered the passageway. "If you're going to take him out, make sure you bonk him RIGHT on the NOGGIN!"

Julius puffed up his chest and pulled the meanest, toughest face he could manage. "Don't you worry about ME!" he said confidently.

I'M JULIUS ZEBRA, CHAMPION OF ROME, SAVIOUR OF BRITANNIA, LIBERATOR OF ENSLAVED BEASTS AND FORMER PHARAOH OF EGYPT!

And with that he tiptoed off into the gloom.

"And those were his last words…" sighed Felix.

Before anyone had a chance to reply, they heard a shuffling noise heading quickly back down the passage. Everyone hastily pulled down their helmets and readied their shields and spears.

"It's only me!" whispered Julius. "Put your pointy spears down!"

"Did you see him?" asked Felix.

"Yes," replied Julius.

"He's at least ten times bigger than that hairy cow we fought in Britannia!" gasped Julius. "There's NO WAY I'm taking him on!"

"Then we should sneak into his lair and try and find the apple without waking him," suggested Lucia.

"Are you volunteering?" asked Milus.

"Er … no …" she replied.

"YOU should go, donkey," growled Milus, pushing Julius forward.

"Me?!" whimpered Julius. "Why me?"

"But he'll eat me alive!" protested Julius.

"If we're lucky," snarled Milus.

Julius looked over at the snoozing lump that was the Minotaur, then quickly surveyed the mess that surrounded the beast.

"OK," he agreed. "You're right; it was my idea to follow Heracles and I should take responsibility."

Julius stood tall, pulled his helmet down, lifted up his shield and tentatively crept into the waste-strewn chamber.

CHAPTER NINE
LET SLEEPING BULLS LIE

Julius slowly crept around the Minotaur's lair, on the look out for anything apple-shaped. The floor itself was an absolute MESS! *Even worse than the dungeon under the Colosseum*, Julius thought.

Scattered about were bones, rotting food, mangled weapons and ripped armour. Worst of all, there were stinky cowpats everywhere!

This Minotaur truly is a monster!

STINKY COWPAT

Something glinting in the flotsam caught Julius's eye. *It looks small and round,* he thought. *This might possibly be my lucky day!*

Carefully picking his way through the rubbish, Julius sneaked over to the suspicious object. In his haste, he accidentally kicked a small bone which clattered against an old sword. Julius froze as the Minotaur snuffled in his sleep – disturbed, but not disturbed enough to wake.

As Julius was about to move on again, the Minotaur suddenly stirred and rolled over to face the zebra, old bones crunching unpleasantly beneath his solid, muscular body. Fortunately he was still asleep, mumbling to himself as if dreaming.

Julius finally plucked up enough courage to move again. He lifted one hoof slowly over a pile of bones and tiptoed towards the shiny object he'd seen earlier.

Except it wasn't there any more.

Well, that's a bit odd...

Something scurrying to his right caught his eye. Julius turned quickly. The shiny object was running away!

"Hey!" whispered Julius loudly. The Minotaur snorted in his sleep. Ignoring him, Julius tiptoed rapidly towards the scuttling object. Suddenly it leapt into the air and landed on the Minotaur's leg.

Julius stifled a very big scream!

From the other side of the chamber, Felix was
watching what was happening. He patted his pockets.
"Hey! I think that must be Herman, my hermit crab!"
he cried. "The little devil's done a runner!"

"Then you'd better go and retrieve him," ordered
Milus, "before your little friend gets Julius killed!"

Felix hastily scampered towards the Minotaur.
"Herman, you fool, come back here!"

Hearing the commotion, Julius turned to see Felix blundering towards him. Frantically the zebra stuck out his hooves in an attempt to stop the antelope, but it was too late!

For a moment, Julius lay motionless in a pile of bones and cowpats, half-awake, half-concussed.

"D-do you think he heard us?" he burbled.

A great stinking, steaming mass of hair and muscle loomed over Julius.

Julius screamed and went to flee for his life, but the Minotaur stamped his heavy hoof on Julius's tail, clamping him fast to the floor. "WHO ARE YOU THAT DISTURBS MY SLEEP?" bellowed the Minotaur. He thrust his snout into Julius's face; hot, rancid breath blasted Julius's.

The Minotaur roared with indignation and hurled Julius against the stone wall, where he slumped to the dirt floor in a heap.

"Use the string!" called Cornelius helpfully, who was cowering with everyone else in the passageway.

Hearing Cornelius, the Minotaur turned towards the frightened animals and let out a great ROAR in their direction. "I WILL EAT EVERY LAST ONE OF YOU AND PICK MY TEETH WITH YOUR BONES!"

But as the Minotaur leant forward ready to charge, Julius called out boldly to the monster.

"GREAT BEAST! YOU WILL NOT BE DEVOURING ANY BRAVE WARRIORS TODAY!" he cried defiantly.

The Minotaur paused and looked back at the fearless zebra.

"TODAY YOU HAVE MET YOUR MATCH! TODAY, BEAST, YOU FACE ROME'S GREATEST CHAMPION." Julius grasped for his ball of string and held it above his head. "TODAY, YOU HAVE MET **JULIUS ZEBRA!**"

"Oh!" gasped Julius in surprise. "I thought that was meant to take him out!"

The Minotaur lunged at Julius. But, this time, the nimble zebra deftly jumped out of the way.

"Throw it again!" screamed Cornelius.

Julius scrabbled around in the debris, but the ball of string had vanished. "WHERE IS IT?!"

Vaulting off a fallen pillar, Julius was able to dodge the slow-moving Minotaur with ease.

He grabbed the ball from the lumbering creature. *He might be big and horrible*, thought Julius, *but that should make him very SLOW!*

And he was right! Julius waved the ball of string at his friends. "I'VE GOT IT!" But as he held it up triumphantly, he was suddenly jerked backwards off his feet into the rubble on the floor.

"It's still attached to his horns!" cried out Cornelius.

"Hold on a second," said Lucia, jumping up onto the pillar. "I've got a PLAN!" And with that, she leapt into the air and snatched the ball of string out of Julius's hoof.

"WHAT ARE YOU DOING?" shouted Julius. "YOU'LL GET YOURSELF KILLED!"

Lucia landed on a marble plinth with the string held high. "Watch THIS!" she cried.

Cornelius cleverly realized EXACTLY what the wily crocodile was up to. "COME ON, EVERYBODY!" he yelled. "LET'S HELP HER!"

The Minotaur finally collapsed in a heap on the floor, well and truly tangled up.

"Thank you, Lucia!" said a bruised and battered Julius. "What would we do without you?"

"I think we all need to thank YOU!" replied Lucia, dusting off her claws. "That was pretty brave, dashing in here after this brute."

Julius sauntered up to the entangled monster and held his hoof out. "Now just hand over the golden apple, beast," he said calmly, "and we'll be off!"

The Minotaur looked confused. "Golden apple?" he growled. "What are you on about?"

Julius blinked agitatedly. "The golden apple! Heracles, son of Zeus, said it was down here!"

"HERACLES?!" snorted the Minotaur. "What would he know? That blundering buffoon has never set foot down here!"

Cornelius cautiously approached the Minotaur, very confused. "But didn't he come down here and beat you up?" he said. "I thought it was one of his legendary labours."

"I did get beaten up," said the Minotaur sheepishly. "But it wasn't by Heracles – he NEVER does his own labours, the lazy oaf."

Julius nearly choked. "NEVER?!" he spluttered.

"Nah," said the Minotaur gruffly.

"He finds some poor sap to do it for him."

"Like I said, he ALWAYS finds some wallies to do his dirty work," he laughed. "Ah, well, so long as you didn't swear the oath, you'll be all right."

He looked at the group of embarrassed faces in front of him and burst out laughing again. "Ha ha ha! You swore the oath!! Ha ha ha! Hard luck!"

"You really should clean this place up," said a disgruntled Julius. "It's a right old mess!"

"Yeah, all right!" growled the Minotaur. "Who are you, my mum?"

Julius started to trudge back towards the main passageway. "Come on, you lot; let's go."

"But what about the golden apple?" cried Brutus.

"There isn't one," sighed Julius. "And if there is, it was never down here."

The roar of the Minotaur shook the walls of the labyrinth. "I'LL GET YOU, ZEBRA!!!"

Pliny dashed ahead. "That string isn't going to hold him for long, Debra. We should skedaddle!"

"Good point," said Julius. "Milus, do you have the map?"

"YOU CAN'T ESCAPE!!" roared the Minotaur. "IF YOU HAD USED YOUR BALL OF STRING PROPERLY, YOU MIGHT HAVE STOOD A CHANCE!!"

Everyone picked up the pace, tripping over skeletons and banging into walls in their haste.

"Used the string properly?" said Julius. "What does he mean?"

After a panicky twenty minutes, they finally spotted a welcome glint of sunlight ahead.

"We made it!" cried Felix, dashing to the door. "Quick, let's get out of this stupid place!"

The great granite door let out a huge creak as everyone squeezed through the gap and threw themselves outside into the fresh air.

"PHEEYEW!" gasped Julius. "I don't know if I could have put up with that stink for one more second."

That's why you need a seaweed wig: it masks all the smells!

"Yeah," said Pliny, "but what do we get to mask the stink of YOUR HEAD?!"

Julius kicked a skeleton head down the hill in frustration. "This has been an absolute DISASTER!" he moaned. "Not only is there no golden apple, but we've been hoodwinked by that rotter Heracles and now we're all going to be banished to Heebie-Jeebies!"

"Hades," corrected Cornelius.

"That's what I said!"

Before Cornelius could reply, a strange man materialized from nowhere and stood in front of them.

Dear fellows, please excuse the interruption.

"One of your friends, Pliny?" asked Julius.

"Nope," said Pliny. "Never seen him before."

"Gentlemen, I am Theseus, and I have travelled many, many miles." The strange man bowed politely. "I have unfinished business with a certain Minotaur."

Just as he spoke, a distant roar could be heard from behind the door.

"Just through there, mate," said Pliny.

Milus handed him the map. "Take this."

Theseus bowed again. "I am for ever in your debt."

Before he disappeared into the labyrinth, Theseus turned to Julius and Cornelius. "I could not help but overhear that you seek a golden apple."

"Something like that," sighed Julius. "Bit of a lost cause now, though."

Then you must go to the garden of Hesperides...

There you will find many golden apples.

With that, the golden-armoured Greek squeezed through the doorway.

"Wait up!" called out Julius, running after him. "Where was that again?"

Theseus poked his head back round the door. "The garden of Hesperides."

"Hairy Spiders," replied Julius.

"No," repeated Theseus. "Hesperides."

"Hairy Spiders?"

"Hesperides."

"Hairy spiders."

"HESPERIDES!"

"HAIRY SPIDERS!!"

"Repeat after me: Hes..."

"Hairy."

"...perides"

"Spiders."

"Sail west, following the glow of the sun. There you will find the garden of Hairy— Hesperides."

Theseus then looked even more serious. "Oh, as well as the Hesperides nymphs themselves, look out for the hundred-headed dragon!"

"HUNDRED-HEADED DRAGON?!" cried Cornelius.

Forget all that! It looks like we're saved!

We won't have to go to Heebie-Jeebies after all!!

"Yeah, we won't go to hell, but we do get to be eaten by a hundred-headed dragon instead. Wonderful!"

"We need a boat!" Milus pointed out. "Talos smashed our last one, remember?"

Pliny started skipping back down the hill. "Don't you worry about that," said the little mouse. "I've got JUST the thing!"

APPLE WATCH

"Oh, stop yer moaning, Debra," said Pliny. "It gets you to where you wanna be, right?"

"So much for going incognito," growled Milus.

"Whaddya mean?" snapped Pliny. "This boat is the LAST place any Roman will look for you."

"I'll give him that," agreed Julius. "Even a Roman legionary wouldn't be seen dead near this boat."

"I'm STARVING!" cried Brutus, hanging over the ship's side. "I'm so hungry, I could eat my wig!"

"You can blame Milus for that," huffed Cornelius.

We DID have enough biscuits to last us MUCH longer...

Just getting you back for eating all my biscuits in Britannia.

Anyone going to argue? Thought not.

"Well, if we don't see land soon even I will want to eat Brutus's wig," grumbled Julius.

Suddenly, on cue, a cry was heard from the crow's nest.

"LAND HO!" bellowed Rufus. "That posh Greek was right – just follow the glow of the sun!"

"And we'll probably find lots of food too, seeing as it's a garden!" said Julius cheerily.

"I think the only food served in that garden will be US to the million-headed dragon!" said Felix.

"Hundred-headed," corrected Milus.

Using their ever-improving sailing skills, the animals moored up at a small empty jetty they spotted as they entered the harbour.

Surrounding the harbour was a giant grassy slope dotted with little houses and beyond that a small mountain range.

Julius approached one of the many goats standing around eating grass.

"Excuse me, do you know where the garden of Hairy Spiders is, please?" he asked politely.

"HESPERIDES!" corrected Cornelius.

"Sorry!" Julius tried again. "Hairyspuddies! Do you know it?"

The goat looked blankly at Julius while she chewed her cud. "No," she finally replied in a strange accent. "I know not of this place you desire."

But I perhaps know of a goat who does!

She turned to the other goats dotted around the hills behind him. "ARISTOPHONIS!!!" She paused for a second, before shouting again. "ARISTOPHONIS!!!"

One of the goats a few hundred yards away lifted up his head. "Yes?"

"DO YOU KNOW OF THE PLACE THAT IS CALLED..." The goat turned back to Julius and stared at him.

"Oh, er... Hairyspuddies," said Julius nervously. "HAIRYSPUDDIES!"

Aristophonis the goat stood motionless for a while, before skipping over to his shouty friend.

Delphine, do you mean Hesperides?

SKIP!

The first goat looked at Julius. "Do I mean 'Hesperides'?"

Julius looked at Cornelius.

"YES!" shouted Cornelius, exasperated.

"Yes!" said Julius to the goat.

The goat turned to her friend. "Yes, Aristophonis," she said calmly. "That is exactly what I mean."

"Then, Delphine, why did you not say?"

For I know EXACTLY where is this garden that you seek!

And so they headed off into the mountains, led by the two goats.

As they trekked through the rocky terrain, Milus sidled up to Julius. "When they have finished showing us the way, donkey, you won't deny an old friend a well-deserved dinner?" He gave Julius a wink.

"NO, MILUS!" whispered Julius loudly. "You are NOT to eat our new friends!"

Milus tutted and folded his arms in a sulk. "This is going to be TORTURE!"

After a short trek traversing hidden pathways and complicated dirt tracks, they approached a small glade where a warm glow emanated from beyond the trees on the other side.

The two goats gestured towards the small clearing.

"This is where we must leave you," said Delphine. "Through the trees yonder, you shall find the garden that you seek."

Aristophonis stepped forward. "If it is the golden apples that you desire, look for the glow that radiates in the darkness."

"Aren't you coming with us?" asked Julius.

"No," replied Delphine. "There are too many dangers here for a goat, and perhaps for a stripy horse too."

They all slipped behind some bushes and peeked through the branches.

"Now everyone be quiet and get down!" ordered Julius sternly. "We can't mess this up!"

Suddenly Julius spotted some movement among the trees. "There!" he whispered. "I think I saw something!"

Everyone squinted.

"I can't see anything!" grunted Milus. "This is a complete waste of time."

"Yeah!" agreed Brutus sulkily. "There's nothing but trees. You're just making it up!"

Again Julius spotted something shuffling among the trees. "Look! Didn't you see it?" he cried. "Those tree trunks seem to be moving all by themselves!"

"Wait a minute!" gasped Cornelius. "Those aren't tree trunks – they're massive LEGS!!"

Julius slumped down behind his rock and let out a big sigh. "We've had it. There's no way we'll get an apple; we may as well just give up!" He kicked a small stone. "This has been a complete WASTE of time!"

"Hush!" said Lucia, who was still watching the dragon and the glade. "Someone's approaching!"

They watched the man leave. A little while later, a woman came out from the trees, walked past the dragon and up to the parcel.

"Ooh, look!" whispered Lucia. "She must be one of the Hesperides nymphs. I reckon they look after the garden."

"Great," sighed Julius. "Not only do we have to

avoid a huge dragon, but we also have to sneak past some gardeners. This is the worst day of my life!"

Picking up the parcel, the woman approached the dragon and stroked one of his heads.

Suddenly Pliny got very excited. He leapt up onto her rock. "'Ere! That gives me a BRILLIANT idea!" he squeaked.

"Yeah, all right!" hissed Julius. "Keep your hair on; you'll give us away!"

"What is it?" asked Lucia, who always loved a good plan. "Are we dressing up as nymphs?"

"In my spa, I've often heard the locals gabbing about that Trojan Horse malarkey!" continued Pliny more quietly. "Do you know it?"

Julius shook his head. "Nope, sorry, we don't do horses!"

"Yeah!" agreed Brutus, smoothing his wig with his hoof. "Horses are NINCOMPOOPS!"

"It's not a REAL horse!" replied Pliny. "It's a pretend wooden one, which you give to your enemy as a present."

"Hey! We're not here to bump anyone off!" protested Julius in alarm. "We're just here to get an apple!"

"Actually, I think Pliny is on to something!" interrupted Lucia. "We should build the nymphs something like a horse, say a zebra…"

Lucia ignored him and carried on. "We build a big wooden zebra on wheels, then give ourselves away as a present."

"We could write a lovely note!" said Felix.

"Yes," agreed Lucia doubtfully. "I suppose we could."

"ANYWAY!" interjected Lucia. "As Pliny suggested, we should hide inside the zebra, pinch an apple when they're not looking, then roll away to make our escape!"

TROJAN ZEBRA

From the belly of the zebra, little Pliny's head popped out. "Are you coming up then?" he squeaked. "It's proper cosy in here!" He dangled down a rope and Julius climbed up.

Lucia pulled herself up the rope next, followed by Cornelius and Brutus. Poking her head through the trapdoor, Lucia called out to Milus and Rufus.

The two of them leant hard against the big hind legs of the wooden zebra and it began slowly trundling across the dirt paths and grass, until finally they reached the clearing. Milus and Rufus quickly hauled themselves up into the zebra before anyone spotted them.

"Good work, chaps!" said Julius. "Now we just wait until someone comes and gets us!"

They didn't have to wait long. Through the small cracks in the wooden frame, Julius could see two figures approaching the zebra.

"Shush!" he said softly. "Here they come!"

Felix tried to peep through the gaps too, but he couldn't see a thing. "What are they doing?" he whispered, shuffling sideways to get a better glimpse. "Have they found my note?"

"Keep still!" hissed Cornelius crossly. "You'll give us away!"

With a big huff, Felix sat back down.

"My bottom!" complained Felix. "There's a splinter in my bottom!"

"Well, it's going to have to stay there!" said Julius. "Stop shuffling about and KEEP QUIET!!"

Felix tried desperately to pull the splinter out, but to no avail. "It's too small and my hooves are like sausages!" he whimpered.

Suddenly, from his knapsack, Herman the hermit crab crawled out, scuttled up to Felix's bottom and gave it a vigorous pinch.

"Thanks, Herman!" murmured Julius, as the crab scurried back into Felix's knapsack.

Before Julius could reply, everyone was jolted to one side. Then they all fell backwards.

"I think we're moving!" whispered Julius.

Sure enough, when Julius looked through the cracks, he could see that they were trundling out of the glade and into the trees of the garden.

Julius quickly ducked and held up a hoof for silence. "Look out, we're going past the dragon!" he whispered.

Before long, the wooden zebra came to a standstill. At first everyone was too frightened to move, but after about five very long minutes, Julius finally plucked up the courage to look through the cracks.

"Well?" snarled Milus. "There'd better be some apples, or I'm liable to start eating you all."

"Oh, stop being SO dramatic!" chided Lucia.

"Um, I can't see any apples…" admitted Julius. "I also can't see any nymphs."

The other animals peered through various gaps in the wooden zebra.

"Me neither!" said Pliny. "Shall we take a chance and have a mooch around?"

"Bagsy stay here!" said Felix immediately.

"But I thought you hated the splinters?" said Julius.

I hate hundred-headed dragons even more!

"Yeah, I'm with Felix," said Brutus. "I ain't budging either. It's safer in here! "

"Well, if you're staying in here with me," said Felix, "you can get rid of that stinky wig!"

Brutus folded his arms and shook his head. "Wherever I go, my wig goes too!"

"Be quiet!" whispered Julius as he shinned down the rope. Close behind him followed Cornelius, Lucia, Rufus and Milus.

"I'll keep an eye on the wooden zebra!" called out Felix.

"Shh!" hissed Julius. "You lot are SO noisy!"

Julius did a quick scan of the garden before pointing to what looked like a small orchard. "Come on!" he said. "This looks like the place!"

They quickly sprinted to the nearest fruit trees and hid behind the trunks.

"Okey-dokey," said Julius, poking his head out.
"Let's grab an apple and get out of here!"

Everyone crept out from behind their trees and looked up into the branches and down on the ground.

"Wait," said Lucia. "What apples?"

"What do you mean?" replied Julius.

"There AREN'T any!" whispered Lucia.

"Not only are there no apples," said Cornelius, "but there are no LEAVES either!"

"We must be out of season!" cried Cornelius. "Of course! It's early spring and apples don't grow in spring – not even gold ones, I suppose!"

Julius started bashing his head against one of the trunks.

Cornelius grabbed Julius. "Stop that nonsense and come on!"

As they turned to run back to their wooden zebra, they were confronted by a group of nymphs armed with spears and shields.

"Halt, intruders!" cried one of the nymphs. "Are these the scoundrels?"

CHAPTER TWELVE
I KID YOU NOT

Julius and the others were marched into a stinky wooden pen by the nymphs. The hundred-headed dragon lurked in the background, slurping and licking its many lips.

"HOW COULD YOU?!" cried Julius to the traitorous goat. "We thought you were HELPING us!"

Aristophonis chuckled. "For centuries us goats have been fodder for the many-headed dragon," Aristophonis sneered as he trotted around the pen's perimeter. "But I have negotiated a deal with the nymphs: if we goats bring the dragon sufficient food, then we shall be spared."

How fortunate for us that you nincompoops wandered in today!

"Good work, donkey," grumbled Milus, slumped in the corner. "A real hero you've turned out to be."

"Is that so?" fumed Julius, turning on the lion. "Because you've really set a fine example, what with all your constant MOANING and GROANING and SNIPING!"

"Yeah!" chipped in Brutus. "Why DO you hang out with us lot if you hate us all so much?"

"Milus has saved our skins more than once," reasoned Lucia, "so we should be grateful he's with us at all!"

"Yes!" agreed Cornelius diplomatically. "If Milus had wanted to stay with his friends back home, I'm sure he would have!"

Milus curled up into a tight ball like a domestic cat. "What friends?" he muttered to himself gloomily.

"Instead of fighting among ourselves," continued Lucia, "we need to think of a way out of this fix, and FAST!"

As the gang huddled together to thrash out an escape plan, they suddenly became aware of a low, rumbling, rattling sound.

"GOOD WORK, FELIX!" cried Julius. "EVERYONE ABOARD!!"

All the animals leapt out of the pen and one by one they swiftly climbed up the rope into the belly of the zebra.

As Julius and Milus finally climbed aboard, Felix popped his head out. "Come with us, Delphine!"

"No!" she shouted back. "This is my home! And I have a few grievances to settle." With that she angrily confronted Aristophonis. "How dare you betray my goodwill!" she raged. "Those poor animals!"

"Now, now!" protested Aristophonis. "I was only protecting our herd—"

But as he spoke, a great beastly dragon head lunged and grabbed him in its jaws.

Suddenly Milus leapt out through the hatchway and seized the back of the wooden zebra. He shouted to Delphine. "GRAB THE OTHER LEG!"

The goat ran to the other side.

"AIM FOR HIS FOOT!" ordered Milus. Together they both shoved hard.

Swiftly picking up speed, the wooden zebra rolled towards the dragon heading straight for his big gnarly toes!

Rescue mission accomplished, Milus caught up with the trundling zebra and grabbed hold of the dangling rope.

"THANK YOU, MY FRIENDS!" Delphine yelled. "I WILL NEVER FORGET YOU!"

Milus climbed back into the belly of the zebra to a round of applause from his friends.

"Good work, Milus!" cried Julius. "I'm sorry I doubted you!"

Milus shrugged. "Don't worry about it. Just worry about how we're going to stop this ridiculous contraption from rolling off that cliff!"

As the dust settled, the groaning animals hauled themselves out of the wreckage of their wooden zebra.

"Yeah, Milus!" said Pliny. "No need to get so dramatic."

Milus dusted himself down. "Dramatic or not," he huffed, "we're still no closer to finding a golden apple."

Retrieving his wig from the debris, Brutus slapped it back on his head and gave a big harrumph! "Just you wait till I see that Heracles; this whole quest has been one MASSIVE waste of time!"

Julius swatted his brother's hoof away. "I think you're forgetting that YOU couldn't stop yourself pleading with Heracles to give you immortality either!"

"Only because YOU were so keen!" retorted Brutus. "But we've been completely HAD!"

Brutus started to walk away from the wreckage. "That rotter saw you coming a MILE off!" he huffed. "EVERYTHING you do is a disaster! You should have 'LOSER' tattooed on your forehead and save us from getting into any more trouble!"

He looked back at Julius. "With you, anything that COULD go wrong DOES go wrong."

Julius ran after Brutus and rugby-tackled him to the ground. "WHY, YOU UNGRATEFUL—!"

"Yeah!" replied Brutus. "Except everything Julius touches turns to RUBBISH!"

Cornelius slapped his forehead. "That's IT!" he exclaimed. "Brutus, you're a GENIUS!"

"Now WAIT ONE MINUTE!" Julius protested. "He was being an absolute MEANIE just then!"

"I know, I know!" replied Cornelius. "But he may have just saved the day, and our friend Heracles too!"

Julius was confused. "Cornelius, what are you BLATHERING on about?"

"Isn't it obvious?"

We pay a visit to King Midas!

CHAPTER THIRTEEN
GET KNOTTED

The journey to Midas City was a tetchy, awkward affair. Brutus had made Julius feel like a failure, and being stuck on a tiny ship with someone grumpy is not ideal at the best of times.

Julius looked wistfully up at the sail as it fluttered in the wind. "I had hoped these adventures would bring us closer. Brutus has his moments of pig-headedness, but then he seems to come round and actually be a good friend as well as a brother."

Cornelius patted his friend comfortingly on the back. "You're younger than him, and then he sees you getting on so well in the world. Of course he's going to lash out! He's jealous."

"Perhaps he's right, though," sighed Julius. "Maybe I have made an almighty mess of things."

Forget about him.

Once we find King Midas, he'll soon come around.

"Are you sure we're going the right way, Pliny?" called out Cornelius. "It's been two days since our stopover at Crete."

"Yes! Not far now!" squeaked Pliny. "A few more hours, then we should reach the port of Attalea." He skipped over to Julius and Cornelius. "We have to be

EXTREMELY careful, though. Attalea is a very Roman port these days. They say Hadrian himself visited not so long ago."

He pulled on a hooded top. "We'll have to be properly disguised," he told them, tugging the hood low over his face. "You lot stay on the ship, while I buy us a horse and cart for the five-day trip to Phrygia, where we'll find Midas's palace."

Five days!

We'll barely make it back in time to meet up with Heracles!

IF he shows up at all!

As Pliny told them, it was another few hours before they finally reached Attalea. Everyone hid below deck, while Pliny scampered off to find them transport.

"Wait there, I won't be long!" the little mouse ordered.

As Pliny skipped off, Julius poked his head up above deck to have a peep at the port. But, with a yelp, he quickly ducked back down.

"What is it?" asked Lucia.

"Pliny wasn't kidding!" gasped Julius. "There are Romans EVERYWHERE!"

Rufus poked his head up to have a look too.

"WHAT?!" cried Julius.

"SHH!" warned Cornelius. "Now's definitely not the time to draw attention to ourselves!"

"Too late!" said Rufus, quickly withdrawing his neck. "Someone's coming!"

"Pliny?"

"Romans!"

Everyone sat very still, listening out for any noise. Suddenly there was a sharp rap on the side of the ship.

"Hello?" called a voice. "We need to see your papers!"

"We've had it!" whispered Felix. "They'll throw us to the lions!"

Footsteps thumped on the deck above their heads. As everybody froze, Lucia suddenly leapt up. "I've got this!" she whispered.

The two soldiers drew their swords and pointed them at the crocodile.

"We need to see your papers," said one sternly. "You have to have a licence to moor here."

"Oh, boys, boys!" Lucia clapped. "You both look so stressed!" She pointed to the big adverts on the side and sail. "You have definitely come to the right boat!"

Before they could answer, she grabbed one of the soldiers and made him lie face down flat on the deck.

The second soldier looked on, just as bemused. "'Ere, can I have a go next? I've got a right old stiff neck!"

"Of course, of course!" replied Lucia. She turned to the hatch. "PERHAPS ONE OF MY ASSISTANTS COULD HELP?"

There was the sound of scuffling and whispers of "You go!" and "No, YOU go!" before the familiar face of Milus popped up above deck.

"How may I be of service?" he snarled.

Suddenly little Pliny jumped on board carrying a bundle of blankets. He nearly fainted at the sight before him.

The soldiers hastily pushed Lucia and Milus away, jumped up and drew their swords on Pliny.

"IS THIS YOUR BOAT? WHERE ARE YOUR PAPERS?"

Pliny rushed to placate them. "Gentlemen! Calm down!" he said. "I see you have sampled our world-famous services."

I can waive our usual fees ...

... if you'll allow me some time to gather the papers that you need.

The two soldiers looked at each other, then back at Pliny. "You've got half an hour, mouse," barked one of them, "and when we return, I want you to do my feet!" He leant into Pliny's face. "DO I MAKE MYSELF CLEAR?"

"As a bell!" replied Pliny. "Your feet will love you for ever!"

As the two soldiers left the ship, Pliny fell into a heap on the floor.

Julius jumped up on deck. "Good work, you three!" he laughed. "I thought we were goners for sure!"

Pliny picked up the blankets and threw them at his friends. "Put these over your heads and come with me. We have to get out of here before those soldiers come back." He leapt off the boat and started to head up the road. "Hurry! This way! I've got us a cart and a couple of horses!"

Down an old back alley, they found two horses reined to a cart.

"Jump in the back and I'll chuck that big blanket over you!" said Pliny. "We'll be safe once we're out of the city."

CHAPTER FOURTEEN
DON'T GET TOUCHY

Once past the city walls, the journey was Roman-free. Apart from the odd traveller and gang of bandits, the animals' ride was plain sailing.

As they trundled along in their cart through a particularly dense stretch of forest, Julius jumped up and clapped his hooves together.

"Now listen up, everyone!" he called. "I know things have been tough, and you were probably all expecting this to be over by now."

"ANYWAY!" said Julius. "We only have a few hours of journey left, so I think, to celebrate, we should have a SING-SONG!!"

"Can we not sing zebra songs?" protested Pliny. "We ALWAYS sing stupid zebra songs!"

Julius put up his hooves. "You can sing whatever you like! Even mouse songs!"

They all sat there thinking for a moment, racking their brains for a good song.

Suddenly, out of Felix's knapsack, crawled little Herman the hermit crab. He scuttled along the side of the cart and stopped at the back on top of a bale of hay.

He perched there silently for a moment, then nervously cleared his throat. He tapped his claws to get a rhythm, then burst into song.

"One, two, three, four, five, once I caught a fish alive!"

"This is the STUFF!" laughed Julius. "All hail HERMAN THE HERMIT CRAB!"

As they whiled away the next few hours with all sorts of merry songs, the forest began to thin out until they could finally see a gleaming white and gold palace on the hillside ahead.

"Ooh!" cried Julius. "That MUST be it!"

Everyone turned to look.

As they climbed the steep hill, they drove their cart up to the huge wooden doors of the perimeter wall.

Julius jumped out and examined the colossal doors. "What do we do?" he asked. He turned to the others and gave a shrug. "Just knock?"

Milus remained unconvinced by the whole plan. "I still say this is ridiculous," he growled. "What are we going to do when we see him? Say 'Excuse me, do you mind turning an apple into gold, please? Thank you!'"

Lucia was less than convinced too. "What if he doesn't even have the power? What if it's all some stupid legend? Heracles is hardly living up to his legendary status so far."

"Yeah!" chimed in Felix. "He might have us EXECUTED just for ASKING!"

A huge creak interrupted Felix's whining and a guard looked out.

"Who dares knock on the doors of MIDAS?"

"See! I told ya!" whispered Felix, lying low in the cart. "We're all for the CHOP!"

The guard looked Julius up and down, cast a glance at the frightened animals in the cart, then looked back at Julius again.

"Wait here," he commanded, and he disappeared, closing the doors firmly behind him with a great BOOM!

Julius turned back to his friends and gave another shrug.

After ten long minutes, the doors once again opened, making Julius nearly jump out of his skin.

The soldier stood proudly by the open doorway. "His Majesty, King Midas, welcomes Lord Julius and his companions and invites them to dine with him this evening."

With the cart in tow, Julius entered a grand courtyard, with flagstones of many fantastic and intricate patterns. Dotted everywhere were trees and plants of all shapes and sizes and colours. Occasionally, sat amongst the plants, golden objects glinted in the sun. Everyone climbed out of the cart to take a closer look, only to find perfectly carved and realistic golden animals that seemed like they would jump at you at any moment.

"Check out these ornaments!" said Julius. "This squirrel looks so real."

"Come," ordered the guard. "Do not delay any further. The king awaits."

He led them down a long passageway, away from the courtyard, golden statues lined up on either side.

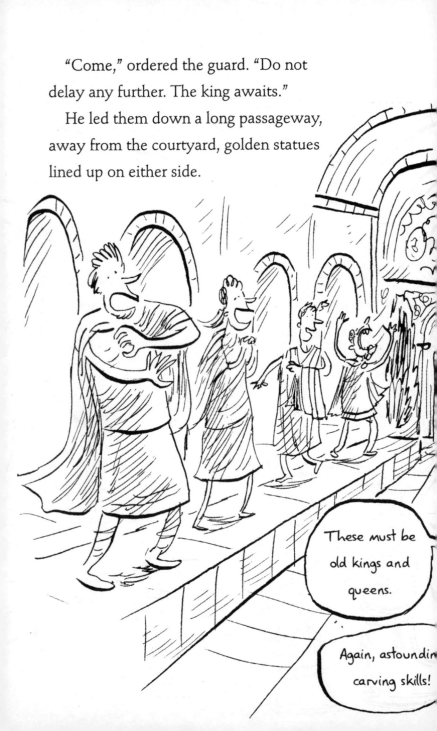

These must be old kings and queens.

Again, astoundin carving skills!

Cornelius was also eyeing the statues as they walked. "Is it just me, or are their poses a bit weird?" he muttered quietly to Julius.

"How do you mean?"

"Well," continued the little warthog, "normally a statue is a celebration of somebody in a regal pose, you know – waving, or looking important."

Julius and Cornelius looked at each other in horror as the penny finally dropped. They slowly stepped away from the statue and hurriedly caught up with the rest of the party who had arrived at some grand ornate double doors. The guard banged on one with the hilt of his sword. The heavy thumping echoed down the pasageway and around the cavernous palace.

Almost immediately, the doors swung open to reveal a magnificent-looking banquet hall with an impressive long table down the middle with cutlery and crockery already laid out.

A young, bearded man greeted them. "Come in! Come in!" He was dressed in smart, colourful woven robes and wore a shiny golden crown.

"What an honour!" he declared. "What. An. HONOUR!"

He made a beeline towards Julius and held out his hand to greet him. "It's very exciting to meet you, Lord Julius." Immediately Julius flinched and pulled his hoof away.

Julius hastily grasped the king's hand and shook it vigorously. "No, no!" he said. "The pleasure is all mine! All mine!"

Felix turned to Brutus. "Why are they repeating everything?" he whispered.

"It must be the posh way of doing things," replied Brutus.

Meanwhile, in his nervousness, Julius had gripped King Midas's hand so tightly that when Midas withdrew his hand, the glove was left in Julius's clenched hoof.

"Come, come!" said the king, slipping his glove back on as if nothing had happened. He motioned to the huge table. "Take a seat. You are obviously exhausted from your arduous journey!"

"Yes, sorry, sorry," stammered Julius. "We, er …
met lots of bandits on the way. My nerves are a bit
on edge."

"Of course," replied the king graciously.

As everyone pulled out a chair, King Midas clicked
his gloved fingers and food was immediately served.

"A king must ALWAYS be prepared!" said Midas.
He snapped his fingers again and a small group of
musicians gathered in one corner and began playing
traditional Greek folk music.

"Oh, how lovely!" slurped Felix through a
mouthful of food. "We were only having a sing-song
ourselves half an hour ago, weren't we, Julius?"

"Oh, really?" asked the king. "Pray tell what tunes you have brought from Rome and Egypt!"

"Do you know the one about a fish being caught alive?" replied Felix.

"Not now!" interrupted Julius hastily. "King Midas doesn't want to hear about your hermit crab's nonsense!"

"Perhaps later," said the king, still excited to receive guests in his palace. "Tell me about YOU, Lord Julius." He smiled at Julius. "Your fame has reached even these remote hills of Phrygia!"

Midas took a sip of his wine. "Is it true you have bested that Roman scoundrel Hadrian TWICE, and ruled Egypt to boot? Very impressive, I must say."

The banquet hall went very quiet as Julius choked on the lettuce leaf he was chewing. "GOSH, NO!" he spluttered. "Not at ALL!" He grabbed a napkin and nervously wiped his face.

The king stared intently at Julius, before breaking into a smile, then a chuckle, then outright laughter. "HA HA HA HA HA HA!!!" he roared, slapping Julius on the back. "YOUR FACE! IT WAS A PICTURE!!"

Julius and his friends all began laughing nervously along, looking sideways at one another, wondering what the joke was.

"Ha ha har!" laughed Julius weakly. "You got me there!"

The king suddenly stopped laughing. "But tell me honestly – why ARE you here?"

What brings the superstar Julius Zebra to my halls?

"Well, you know," said Julius, popping another lettuce leaf into his mouth and glancing anxiously at his friends. "We were on our holibobs in Greece…"

"Holibobs?" repeated a confused Midas.

"Yeah, holibobs," confirmed Julius. "We saw a bit of Crete, went to a spa."

Pliny gave a wave. "My spa!"

Midas raised an eyebrow and nodded in approval.

"And we wondered," continued Julius, "what great Greek legend should we visit?"

"What indeed!" agreed Midas.

"And we all said, 'Yeah, what a brilliant idea!' and so here we are!"

"Well, I am glad you did and I thank you for the company." Midas raised his glass before taking another sip.

He flopped back in his chair with a sigh. "We don't get many visitors," he said, "but my burden" – and he held up a gloved hand – "or should I say my CURSE does rather lure the curious…"

The banquet hall fell silent again.

"So, er, the stories *are* true," asked Julius. "You are truly cursed with a golden touch?"

Midas gazed at Julius, a scornful look in his eye. "Yes," he whispered. "And it's not easy."

He held up one hand. "These lead-lined gloves help, but they cannot always be trusted to stave off the curse."

"You know," said Midas, "the worst of it – and you'll understand this, Julius – is people

DEMANDING I turn things to gold, like I'm some sort of performing MONKEY!"

Julius laughed nervously. "Oh, er, crikey! Ha ha ha!" he stammered. "That must be AWFUL!"

"You probably saw my collections of those who dared ask me to perform such a trick!"

Julius risked a frightened sideways glance at Cornelius.

At that moment, across the table, Brutus stood up holding a big green apple in his hoof. "Saying that, though," he began, flipping the apple into the air and catching it again.

"Yes?" asked Midas, a frown furrowing his brow.

"You see this apple?"

"What of it?" growled Midas.

"BRUTUS!" shouted Julius. "Not now!"

Brutus has his own party trick of stuffing an apple in his mouth and shutting up for the rest of the evening!

Gluh!

"Interesting…" Midas murmured.

"ANYWAY!" cut in Julius, raising his goblet. "Let's drink to us poor celebrities and our troublesome fans!"

Draining his goblet, Midas stood up and began suddenly swaying to the jolly folk music. "Come, Julius!" he cried. "Dance with me!"

Julius choked on his food again. "What?! REALLY?"

"YES! YES!" laughed Midas. "ALL of you! Here in Phrygia it is customary to dance after dinner!"

"This I gotta see!" scoffed Milus, slouching in his chair.

"You too, lion!" insisted Midas, roughly dragging the reluctant beast up onto his feet.

CHAPTER FIFTEEN
GOLDEN BOY

"What time is it?" asked Julius.

Cornelius looked out of the nearest window at the stars. "Almost certainly past midnight."

"This is probably the latest I've EVER stayed up," yawned Julius.

In the corner, the musicians were still playing their folk songs and Felix, Pliny and Rufus were throwing mad shapes in a desperate attempt at Greek dancing.

"Guys!" called out Julius. "Give those poor musicians a rest and come and sit down!"

The animals reluctantly came back to the table and sat down, while the musicians packed up, made their farewells and left for bed.

Brutus, sitting opposite his brother, leant over the table and whispered, "So, are we going to do it now, or what?"

"Do what?" Julius whispered back, holding up a hoof to shush him.

"Duh! Get him to touch an apple!" said Brutus. "Why else are we here?"

"You heard the man," hissed Julius. "He doesn't like being asked to use his powers. Did you see those 'statues' outside? We'll just have to find another way."

Brutus huffed and flopped back into his chair. He glared for a while at Julius while popping grapes into his mouth. Suddenly he leapt up onto the table, grabbed an apple and made a beeline for the snoozing Midas.

Brutus hopped off the table beside Midas. "I'm going to do it!" he declared. "We've not travelled hundreds of miles just to dance to weird music!" Bending down beside Midas's chair, he started to tug at one of the king's gloves.

Julius was beside himself with distress. "BRUTUS!" he hissed loudly. "Step away now, or I'll not be responsible for my actions!"

Milus bounded onto the table and thrust a spear towards Brutus.

Brutus looked cooly at Milus, then, with a swift flick, pulled the glove off and tossed it over his shoulder.

Everyone let out a gasp as Milus's spear pressed against Brutus's throat. Without breaking sweat, Brutus slowly held up a golden, gleaming apple. "There!" he said, throwing it to Milus. "It's done. Now we can go!"

Milus inspected the apple. "That is actually quite impressive, donkey." He threw it to Julius.

Julius also examined the apple, then looked up crossly at Brutus. "You blithering idiot! You'll be the end of us!"

He stuffed the apple into his tunic pouch and stood up slowly from his chair. Luckily Midas was still fast asleep.

Felix and Rufus trotted over to have a look. "Show us how you did it!" begged Felix. "We want to see!"

"No!" said Julius emphatically. "We're in enough trouble. We need to GO!"

Ignoring him, Felix grabbed a banana from the fruit bowl and touched it against Midas's bare finger.

Not wanting to be left out, Rufus searched for something else to turn into gold. He quickly grabbed Brutus's stinky seaweed wig and brushed it against Midas's hand. The wig turned to solid gold.

"Hey, you rotter, that's mine," protested Brutus, but as he went to grab it back his hoof caught Midas's thumb and he turned instantly into a statue of gold.

As they all stood frozen in shock, the huge doors opened and the guard from earlier walked in. "The guest rooms are ready—" He stopped in his tracks, taking in the scene before him. "WHAT IN THE NAME OF—"

"We have to go now, or we're ALL dead."

CHAPTER SIXTEEN
HE AIN'T HEAVY...

Julius, Milus and Rufus all grabbed hold of Brutus and heaved him towards the door.

"This is ridiculous!" cried Julius. "He weighs a flippin' TON!"

Lucia ran to one of the long red velvet curtains hanging at the grand windows and ripped it from its pole, sending curtain rings flying everywhere.

She dragged the curtain over to Brutus. "Lay him on here," she said.

As they dragged Brutus through the doors and out into the corridor, Midas began to stir. "Wh-where's everyone gone...?" he murmured drowsily.

Lucia and Rufus slammed the doors shut and Lucia slipped her spear through the handles, sealing the doors.

"LOOK AT THE DOORS!" cried Rufus.

Everyone spun round to see what the giraffe was shouting about.

"THEY'VE TURNED GOLD!" squealed Cornelius.

A great roar erupted from the banquet hall as Midas realized what had happened.

"WAIT TILL I GET MY HANDS ON YOU!"

he bellowed. "YOU'LL BE STANDING IN MY STATUE COLLECTION WITH THE REST OF THE THIEVING SCOUNDRELS!"

"Can't we move him any quicker?" panted Julius. "I don't want to end up as a statue too!"

"We've got to get him down these steps first!" said Lucia.

"Try not to break him!" panicked Julius. "I know he's an idiot, but he's MY idiot!"

They gently placed Brutus on the top step.

"Now, be gentle," said Julius. "One step at a time!"

Everyone kneeled behind Brutus and waited for the command.

"Hurry up!" urged Cornelius. "His guards will be here any second!"

"One," continued Julius, "two ... THREE!"

Everyone raced after the gold Brutus, trying to catch him before he did any more damage.

"GRAB HIM!" cried Julius. "HE'LL LOSE A NOSE OR AN ARM OR SOMETHING!"

As the rolling Brutus reached the doors at the end, three guards suddenly appeared. "STOP, OR FACE DEATH!" they shouted.

Julius clapped. "Good work, Brutus!"

"Is it me," said Milus, "or is Brutus far more useful as a statue than as a living, breathing zebra?"

Everyone rushed through the smashed doors to discover Brutus had finally come to a stop in the middle of the courtyard.

"Where's our ride?" panicked Julius. "We have to get out of here quick!"

"Stop worrying!" said Pliny, leaping into action. "Watch this!"

Almost immediately, the horses and cart pulled up out of nowhere.

"Good work!" cried Julius in relief.

"All horses and carts come with a free whistle upgrade these days," revealed Pliny. "We're truly living in the future!"

Once Brutus was finally loaded, everyone else jumped on and Pliny flicked the reins. "Giddy up!" he cried. "Back to port for us!"

As they zipped off, they heard a voice yelling at them from behind.

"As if we weren't in ENOUGH trouble with Rome!" sighed Julius. He rested his hoof on the frozen golden figure of Brutus. "Oh, brother, what trouble you have brought upon us..."

"Well, he did do ONE good thing before he ... er ... went," said Cornelius.

Julius didn't look up from stroking his poor brother. "No, Cornelius," he said quietly. "This quest is far from over."

"What do you mean?" Cornelius exclaimed. "We have the apple!"

"Yes, but I've lost my brother," replied Julius. "And I intend to get him back!"

"Get him back? HOW?"

"If my brother is dead, then he must already be in Hades."

CHAPTER SEVENTEEN
JOURNEY TO THE UNDERWORLD

Sailing to the fabled underworld hadn't been the easiest of tasks, but Julius remembered Heracles saying that he'd heard of people being rescued from there, so he knew it was possible.

After much searching and asking around in Attalea, then back in Pliny's home of Crete, the animals had managed to track down an old map that purportedly showed the way to Hades.

This really is a long shot, Julius. Any fool could have drawn this!

"I know," replied Julius, "but it's all we have." He looked out towards the darkening storm clouds. "If Heracles says people can be rescued from Hades, then we have to try!"

A chill wind blew across the sea, and on deck everyone pulled their blankets tighter over their heads and shoulders. They had reached the mouth of a dark river that was marked on their map.

The river twisted and turned through a forbidding, misty landscape, as haggard crows cawed at them from rotten trees. Everyone clutched their swords tighter, ready for any danger.

As they slowly sailed round another bend, the river widened to reveal the mouth of a pitch-black lake.

"I DEFINITELY think we've found the right place," gasped Felix.

In the distance was a jetty with a small boat moored at one end.

Cornelius glanced at the map. "Head for that jetty," he ordered.

That's where we'll find the ferryman!

They climbed out onto the creaky, ramshackle pontoon.

"Be careful!" Julius warned. "These planks are falling apart!"

They gingerly walked across to the small rowing boat with its mysterious passenger.

Julius approached the hooded figure warily. "Excuse me, are you the ferryman?"

Cornelius consulted his map again. "He's called Charon," he whispered.

Julius cleared his throat. "Are you the one they call Sharon?"

The figure didn't speak or move. Only the gentle lapping of the water broke the silence.

Julius turned to the others and shrugged. He tried again. "Excuse me—"

His icy voice floated on the breeze from the lake.

Charon.

Julius pulled his blanket tighter around his shoulders and let out a little *brrr*. "I'm sorry," he said. "What did you say?"

There was a pause, before another icy whisper drifted from the hood. "My name is *Charon*."

"I have an Auntie Sharon!" piped up Felix.

Julius turned round and put his hoof to his mouth to shush Felix.

"Listen, Sharon," said Julius carefully. "I need to cross this lake to find my brother and I've been told that you can help me."

In reply, Charon held out a bony hand.

Gasp! He's a skellybob!

"He needs paying!" said Cornelius.

Julius showed him the golden apple. "Will this do?"

"No, Julius!" hissed Cornelius. "Give him a coin."

"This is all I've got," replied Julius. "And there's no point in keeping it if I can't have my brother back."

Julius carefully placed the golden apple in Charon's hand.

Charon raised the apple to his hood and held it there as if examining it. He then set it beside him.

There was a long, awkward pause.

"Is that a yes?" asked Julius eventually.

"I think that's a yes!" said Cornelius.

Once they were all settled, Charon began slowly rowing across the great expanse of lake.

As they glided across the lake, Julius was amazed at how still the surface was. The only ripples came from their boat. There was not a sound to be heard: no birds in the sky, no rustling of the wind. Only the gentle splash of the oars dipping in the water broke the silence.

Before long, a dark shadow of land loomed menacingly through the mist. As they drew closer, Julius saw that it was a mountainous, foreboding land, devoid of colour and life. Dead, gnarly trees sat among ravaged boulders.

This looks like a fun place.

Charon stopped rowing as they glided to the shore, and everyone stepped off into the shallows and made their way to dry land.

The ferryman reached out as Julius passed and seized him by the arm.

Through there, you will find your brother.

He tugged Julius closer. "Take this lyre," he hissed, passing him a small stringed instrument. "It will soothe the darkest of souls."

Julius went to move away, but Charon held onto him tight. "Once you find your brother," he hissed, "do not look back at him as you pass back through the gate, not until you reach my boat."

"Thank you, Sharon," gulped Julius.

CHAPTER EIGHTEEN
SPIRITED AWAY

"Right," said Julius, walking up the hill, "let's get this over and done with as quickly as possible. I don't want to stay in this place any longer than I have to."

He pointed to the gate in the distance. "Sharon says we'll find Brutus through there, so let's go!"

Felix held up a smooth round grey stone. "You can't visit the netherworld and not collect a rock. I wouldn't be able to forgive myself!"

In the corner of Julius's eye, a shadow flitted between the rocks and trees behind Felix.

"Well, if you want to stay here with all the ghosts and ghoulies," said Julius, "then that's up to you!"

Felix spun round to see the lurking figure and hastily stood up and plopped his stone in his knapsack.

They dashed towards the others, who were crouched down near the ancient, crumbling stone gate.

Julius ran up the path right past them. "Come on!" urged Julius. "What are you all doing hiding behind those rocks? Let's not dilly-dally!"

Wait! There seems to be some sort of big dog guarding the gate!

"Big dog?!" blurted out Julius, as he skidded to a halt on the gravel. He ran back to where Cornelius was hiding behind a boulder. "Sharon never mentioned anything about a guard dog!"

"This is no ordinary dog, either," said Cornelius.

"But there are seven of us," exclaimed Julius. "Surely we can tackle a single dog between us?" Julius suddenly heard a loud snuffling and low growling coming from the gate. He decided to have a peek around the boulder to see exactly what it was.

"Well, that's that then!" said Julius slumping against the boulder. "We're not getting past THAT thing!"

Brutus is lost forever. Mum is going to KILL me!

Lucia came and sat next to her friend. "Come on, Julius; there's ALWAYS a way!"

Julius appreciated the sentiment, but he shook his head. "I know you can usually find a way out of a tight spot, Lucia, but I think we've had it this time."

Lucia wasn't having any of it. She picked up the lyre that Charon had given him. "What's this for?" she asked.

"Oh, Sharon says to play this to 'soothe the darkest of souls' or something."

"Huh!" replied Lucia, and she started plucking at the strings. A beautiful tune began to play by itself.

Sitting on a boulder next to them, Milus immediately fell asleep and began snoring.

"'Ere! What happened to grumpy guts?" asked Pliny, pointing at Milus. "He's dropped right off!"

Julius took the lyre and held it up to have a good look. "That. Is. AMAZING!"

Good work, Lucia!

Maybe this will do the trick!

Julius carefully crouched behind a large boulder further up the path and waited for the big dog to come his way as it paced up and down in front of the gate. As soon as the snuffling and growling grew louder, Julius leapt out in front of the beast and began playing the lyre.

The big dog came to a halt and the beast's eyelids began to droop. The soothing sound of the lyre seemed to be doing the trick!

Eager to speed things up, Julius decided to sing along to the melody.

Unfortunately, Julius's nasal caterwauling only served to wake the creature from its drowsiness. With a great ROAR, it shook its three heads and turned to Julius, its eyes red with fury.

"STOP SINGING!" squealed Cornelius. "YOU'RE UPSETTING HIM!!"

"You're upsetting me too!" complained Pliny, his paws stuffed in his ears.

"Well, HOW rude!" huffed Julius, but he stopped his warbling and let the lyre play on its own.

Once again, the monster dog started to relax, and finally it flopped to the ground in a sluggish slumber.

Julius sneaked over just to make sure.

He motioned everyone to come forward and they all tiptoed past the snoozing beast.

Once through the gate, they discovered a world of ancient crumbling ruins among the long-dead trees. The fog was thicker and gloomier here and the cold, damp air chilled their bones.

"How on Earth are we going to find him out HERE?" wailed Julius. In desperation, he called out his brother's name.

Julius's voice echoed through the murkiness, but no reply came. Some of the others began calling out Brutus's name too as they wandered through the mist.

But, as all seemed lost, Rufus suddenly cried out from a clump of gnarled tree stumps just ahead.

"Over here, Julius!" he cried. "I think I can see someone!"

Everyone ran towards Rufus and, sure enough, a shadowy figure seemed to be walking towards them through the gloom.

"Brutus?!" called out Julius excitedly. "Is that you?"

As the animals turned to flee, they saw more skeletons marching towards them, each dressed up in decayed tunics and armour.

"WILL YOU PLEASE KEEP THE NOISE DOWN!!" they bellowed, waving their rusty swords and spears.

As fearsome as it looked, the skeleton army was fortunately no match for Julius and his well-trained friends.

"This is easy-peasy!" laughed Rufus, as he bashed up two flimsy skeletons at once.

Lucia was leaping off the ruins and knocking the undead into countless pieces. "Yes, but there's SO many of them!"

But poor Julius was starting to get frantic. "This is distracting us from our mission!" he cried. "We need to lose this skeleton horde!"

"I'm with you!" said a familiar voice.

Julius gave his long-lost brother a big hug.

"'Ere!" protested Brutus, trying to push him off. "What are you doing?!"

"What am *I* doing?" laughed Julius. "What are YOU doing?! How did you find us?"

"I'm not sure," admitted Brutus, rubbing his head. "One minute I'm turning apples into gold, the next I'm stuck here in this rotten place with this stinky lot!"

As he pushed the skeleton away, Brutus grabbed Julius desperately by the shoulder. "Brother, where IS this place?"

"Best not to ask!" replied Julius. "Come on, we've got to go!"

Julius jumped onto a big boulder and held up his sword. "Everyone, great news! I've found Brutus!" he announced. "Let's leave these skellybobs and head back to Sharon!"

As the others ran off, a tired Brutus found himself caught up in a tangle of skeletons. "JULIUS!" he cried breathlessly. "DON'T LEAVE WITHOUT ME!"

Julius turned back and hauled him out of the bony mêlée. "This way, Brutus. I'm not about to lose you twice!"

Throwing his arm around his brother, Julius led Brutus away from the skeleton mob and towards the giant stone gates. As they approached the gateway, Julius hid cautiously to the side.

"Careful here," Julius warned. "We have to watch for a big three-headed guard dog!" He peered around the crumbling column. "Hopefully he's still asleep."

But, before Julius crossed the gate threshold, he remembered Charon's warning.

Do not look back to your brother when you pass through the gate, not until you reach my boat.

Julius took a deep breath before running out through the gateway and past the snoring monster dog. "This way, Brutus!" he called out careful not to look back. "We're nearly there!"

But Brutus didn't reply.

Julius started to panic. *What if he's been recaptured by the skellybobs?* he thought. *How am I supposed to help him if I'm not allowed to look back at him?* But Julius didn't look back, or who KNOWS what would happen. He tried calling out to his brother again, "Hey Brutus, can you imagine what Mum's going to say after we tell her about our mad adventures?" he laughed. "She'll go spare, eh, Brutus?"

Again, no reply.

It was no good, Julius couldn't bear it. *What if my brother really is in trouble?* he thought. *I couldn't live with myself if I left him behind in this rotten place!* Julius stopped running. *What's the worst that could happen if I looked back, anyway?*

So he turned round. "Brutus, are you all right?"

And there, right as rain, was Brutus. He was running right behind him, deep in concentration, and picking his nose.

Suddenly, as Brutus wiped his bogey on a nearby rock, he started to turn a strange greyish blue colour. "'Ere! What's happening?!" he cried.

Brutus reached out his hoof to Julius, but, like a wisp of smoke slowly dispersing in the wind, he was gone.

❦ CHAPTER NINETEEN ❦
JOURNEY'S END

Julius dejectedly walked back to the boat.

"Where's Brutus?" asked Cornelius.

"Gone," replied Julius.

"Gone?" gasped Cornelius. "Gone where?"

Julius climbed aboard the boat and slumped against the side.

"Yeah, all right," snapped Julius. "No one likes a know-it-all."

Lucia jumped up and unsheathed her sword. "Well, what are we waiting for?" and she leapt into the water and waded to the shore. "Let's get him back!"

Charon let out an icy hiss. "None that are living may pass through the gates of Hades twice."

Everyone shivered as Charon's icy words chilled the air.

"I bet he's a right laugh at parties," whispered Pliny to Milus.

Lucia reluctantly returned to her friends and Charon rowed the little boat back across the lifeless lake.

"We've completely failed," sighed Julius. "Not only have we lost Brutus, but we don't even have the golden apple!"

They finally reached the shore and were glad to see their ship was still there waiting.

Julius thanked Charon and they all made their way to it and the long journey home. Everyone hopped on board and were about to cast off, when a voice called out to them to wait.

The figure ran along the creaking boards of the pontoon and towards the gangplank. But Julius's heart sank as he realized it wasn't Brutus at all.

"Felix, you bonehead!" cried Julius angrily. "Can't you forget about your ridiculous rock collection for one minute?"

Felix hopped on board and looked put out. "I wasn't collecting rocks!" he protested.

The sail was hoisted and what little wind there was propelled them back towards the River Styx.

But Lucia wasn't having any of it! "This is RIDICULOUS!" she shouted. "We can't just leave Brutus there!" She leapt up and wrested the tiller from Julius's hooves. "Come on, Julius. Forget all that doom and gloom hokey-pokey nonsense from Charon," she said defiantly. "We're going back for your brother and NO ONE is going to stop us!"

"Are we even ALLOWED to do this?" wailed Felix. "Won't Sharon be mad at us?"

"I think that's the least of our troubles," muttered Cornelius, nervously eyeing up the brewing storm clouds overhead.

As they reached the far shore, Lucia vaulted into the water and ran towards the path.

Julius and the others jumped off the boat and paddled ashore. "I've got a really bad feeling about this," whispered Cornelius. "We need to stop her!"

But it was too late. Just as Lucia reached the gate, a great booming voice rumbled through the air.

The ground shook so hard, that everyone fell over.

The deep, loud voice roared in anger. "WHO DARES ESCAPE MY DOMINION, THEN SEEKS TO PASS BACK THROUGH THE GATES A SECOND TIME?"

Lucia ran back to her friends who all lay quivering on the ground.

"Where is that voice even coming from?" asked Felix.

Cornelius, hidden behind a boulder, shakily pointed up to the sky. "Th-th-there!" he stammered.

"That must be Hades himself!" replied Cornelius. "God of the Underworld."

"Hades, god of Hades," said Julius. "That's not confusing at all."

"When I get home," laughed Felix, "I'm going to be Felix, lord of Felix!"

"SILENCE!" bellowed Hades. "YOU ARE THE ONES WHO DARE RUN IN AND OUT OF MY WORLD, WILLY-NILLY!"

YOU SHALL ALL BURN IN THE FIERY RIVER OF ACHERON FOR THIS OUTRAGE!

The giant god held his staff high in the air, then brought it crashing down to the ground. There was a great flash and suddenly the animals found themselves in a metal cage suspended in mid-air.

"NO MERE MORTAL DARES ENTER THE UNDERWORLD TWICE AND LIVES TO TELL THE TALE!" boomed Hades. "FOR THIS CRIME, I SHALL CAST YOU INTO THE PITS OF HELL FOR ALL ETERNITY!"

As Hades held up his staff ready to execute his judgement, Julius squeezed his hooves out of the cage to catch the god's attention. "WAIT! WAIT!" he cried, waving his arms. "We might be mortal, but this is all the fault of an IMMORTAL, like yourself!"

Hades held his staff high in the air, paused for a few seconds, then lowered it back down very slowly.

"SPEAK QUICKLY, HORSE-CREATURE, MY PATIENCE WEARS THIN."

"It was Heracles," cried Julius. "He made us do it!"

"HERACLES?" gasped Hades. "I SHOULD HAVE KNOWN!"

"LABOURS?" asked Hades, slightly confused. "HE FINISHED HIS LABOUR AEONS AGO. WHAT MISCHIEF IS HE UP TO NOW?"

He again raised his staff high in the air and brought it thundering to the ground. A great flash of lightning lit the sky as the ground trembled. Everybody screamed, expecting to be cast into the pits of hell. But much to their relief, they still hung in the air in their cage.

From below, a familiar figure appeared before them.

"That's him!" shouted Julius. "He made us look for a Golden Apple! He said his dad Zoots needed it!"

"How dare you!" replied Heracles. "I WAS looking for it, or I was about to, once I rested my dodgy knee." He waggled his leg for everyone to see. "Look, I twisted it whilst escaping from that terror, Talos!"

"Yes, we found it, no thanks to you!" huffed Julius.

"Then you must give it to me at once!" cried Heracles, reaching desperately towards the cage. "I need it immediately!"

"Well, you're out of luck," snorted Julius. "Thanks to your wild goose chase, we lost my brother to the Underworld."

Heracles looked remorseful. "I am truly sorry," he said. "Your brother was a fine zebra."

"Well, let's not get too carried away..." mumbled Milus.

"So we gave the apple to Sharon!" said Julius.

"Who?!" gasped an enraged Heracles.

"HERACLES, THIS IS NOT THE FIRST TIME YOU HAVE STOOD BEFORE ME ACCUSED OF TREACHERY AND DECEIT!"

"But, Uncle, it wasn't like that, I swear!" pleaded Heracles.

"SILENCE!" roared Hades. "YOU HAVE BEEN WARNED MANY TIMES REGARDING YOUR HABIT OF RUNNING UP DEBTS AND DIRECTING OTHERS TO FIND TREASURES TO PAY YOUR BILLS."

"YOU CANNOT BE ALLOWED TO CONTINUE YOUR ANTICS, SO I HAVE DEVISED A PLAN TO KEEP YOU OCCUPIED," he continued.

"I HAPPEN TO KNOW OF A SECOND LABOUR THAT YOU LEFT INCOMPLETE…"

"NO, HALF-WIT, YOU MUST CLEAN THE AUGEAN STABLES!"

Back in the cage, Julius turned to Cornelius. "Cleaning stables? That's not much of a punishment!"

Cornelius let out a little chuckle. "These stables are different," he replied. "They're cursed with a never-ending supply of poo!"

"Oh, sweet!" laughed Julius.

In the distance, another great flash of lightning crackled across the sky. Heracles was gone.

Hades turned to Julius and his friends once more.

"THE CHARLATAN HAS GONE," said Hades, "AND, AS HIS UNCLE, I APOLOGIZE FOR HIS WRONGS."

"Losing my brother is some 'wrong'," sighed Julius. Hades solemnly waved his staff and the animals found themselves free of the cage and back on the ground.

'Ere, your nephew promised us immortality if we found that apple!

"DID HE, NOW?" replied Hades. He pondered the antelope's words for a while. "BY ALL ACCOUNTS, YOU HAVE BEEN BRAVE IN THE FACE OF ADVERSITY AND CUNNING IN YOUR

ACCOMPLISHMENTS," said Hades. "I CANNOT OFFER YOU IMMORTALITY, BUT I CAN OFFER YOU A REWARD. THINK OF ONE THING THAT YOUR HEART DESIRES AND IT WILL BE YOURS. THIS IS MY GIFT TO YOU AS RECOMPENSE FOR MY NEPHEW'S TRICKERY."

Hades raised his staff and brought it crashing back down to Earth with a flash.

In that instant, Julius and his friends found themselves back home by the lake.

Lucia ran up to Julius, who didn't seem to have a gift of any kind. "Julius!" she said. "What about you? What was your wish?"

Julius pointed to the nearby ridge.

"There!" he said. "That's my gift."

"I'm not sure I'd call bringing that idiot back to life 'a gift'," growled Milus.

Ignoring the lion, Julius gave his brother a big hug. "You might be an idiot," he said. "But you're MY idiot!"

"I'm glad we're all back together again," sighed Julius, sitting down on the grass by the lake. "But after all that craziness, it would've been nice to have something to show for it."

"Yes," lamented Cornelius. "We didn't even get to keep that stupid golden apple.

"Well," interrupted Felix. "That's not entirely true."

Julius nearly fell into the lake with shock. "How on EARTH!?"

"I swapped it for my golden banana," replied Felix. "He was very accommodating."

Cornelius burst into laughter. "You gave Charon, the Ferryman to the Gates of Hell, a Golden Banana?" he cried. "That is amazing! I have a new respect for you, Felix."

"Maybe now we can all afford to open posh spas!" laughed Julius.

🌿 EPILOGUE 🌿

Hadrian sat at his desk admiring the soft, brightly patterned silk he'd been presented as a gift on his latest visit to his Empire's eastern borders.

Magnificent! How I wish my own Empire could create such a divine fabric as this.

A guard suddenly entered the room and saluted his emperor.

"Ave, Caesar!" barked the guard.

"Yes, yes," sighed Hadrian with a huff. "What is it? Can't you see I'm busy?"

"No, I believe they're some kind of mythical dragon," mused Hadrian. "Its true symbolism is still unknown to us..." He quickly rolled the silk up and stuffed it into a desk drawer. "Not that it's any of YOUR business, soldier!" he blustered, suddenly realizing the guard's insolent intrusion. "Now, tell me your news, or you'll find yourself wrestling lions in the Colosseum!"

The soldier stood up straight and coughed nervously. "Ahem ... a Phrygian king seeks your counsel at once, oh Caesar."

Hadrian stood up impatiently. "A Phrygian king?" he scoffed. "I don't have time to chat idly with Phrygian kings!"

Hadrian took a step back. "King Midas ... to what do we owe the pleasure?" He went to put out his hand to greet the king, then recoiled almost immediately.

"I'M WEARING MY GLOVES!" yelled Midas.

"Yes, of course," replied Hadrian and the men shook hands.

"Though, perhaps I ought to disregard such formalities," huffed Midas. "Seeing as Rome deems it necessary to send its greatest champion to STEAL from me and no doubt OVERTHROW me, if my soldiers hadn't had intervened in time."

"Greatest champion...?" repeated Hadrian. "I don't understand."

"The ZEBRA!" roared King Midas. "If it is a war you want on your eastern frontiers, then it's a WAR you'll get!"

Hadrian slumped down onto his chair and rubbed his chin. "The zebra. Of course," he sighed exasperated. "No, it's not a war I want, Midas. But I do want rid of that blasted creature once and for all."

He pulled the exotic silk out from his drawer and rubbed it softly. "And I think I have just the plan..."

❧ ROMAN NUMERALS ❧

Hello readers! Julius has asked me and Felix to help explain the strange page numbers used throughout this book.

Instead of page numbers like 1, 2 and 3, you'll find V, X, I and various other letters, which are Roman numerals — just like the Romans used for counting!

Even an idiot like me can understand them. Hooray!

Here are the seven letters that represent all the Roman numerals.

I = 1
V = 5
X = 10
L = 50
C = 100
D = 500
M = 1000

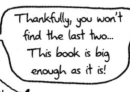

Thankfully, you won't find the last two... This book is big enough as it is!

You simply add Roman numerals together to make different numbers:
II (1 + 1) = 2
VIII (5 + 1 + 1 + 1) = 8
CLI (100 + 50 + 1) = 151

That seems easy enough! I'm off to collect some rocks.

🌿 ROMAN NUMERALS 🌿

WAIT! We're not finished! There are two basic things you need to know to be able to count Roman numerals!

Oh?

1: YOU WILL NEVER FIND MORE THAN THREE ROMAN NUMERALS IN A ROW. 3 is written as III, but 4 is not IIII.

But hold on, how do you write 4 then?

My brain hurts!

2: WHEN A SMALLER NUMERAL COMES BEFORE A LARGER NUMERAL, TAKE AWAY THE VALUE OF THE SMALLER NUMERAL FROM THE BIGGER ONE TO WORK OUT THE NUMBER.

So 9 is IX?

Yes! You can remember it like this: 1 before 10 is 9.

To summarise: Always read Roman numerals from left to right, adding up as you go along. If a larger numeral comes before a smaller or equal numeral, add them together. But if a smaller numeral comes before a larger numeral, take away the value of the smaller numeral from the bigger one before moving on to the next letter in the row.

If there is a next letter, of course!

Here's some to help you along!

1	I	7	VII	13	XIII	50	L	200 CC
2	II	8	VIII	14	XIV	60	LX	300 CCC
3	III	9	IX	15	XV	70	LXX	
4	IV	10	X	20	XX	80	LXXX	
5	V	11	XI	30	XXX	90	XC	
6	VI	12	XII	40	XL	100	C	

GARY'S GLOSSARY

CERBERUS

The three-headed dog who guarded the gate to the Underworld, stopping the dead from leaving and the living from entering. Once kidnapped by Heracles as one of his labours, Cerberus is sometimes depicted with fifty heads and a serpent's tail. Known to enjoy the dulcet tones of a lyre. The rasping caterwauling of a zebra, not so much.

CHARON

The ferryman of the dead who carried souls across the River Styx in exchange for a coin. His name is pronounced more like "Karen" than "Sharon", but let's not let solid facts spoil the author's favourite joke in the book. Pluto's largest moon is named after him.

GOLDEN APPLE

A fruit of Greek legend. It was said that anyone who ate a golden apple would never experience hunger, thirst or illness ever again. Coveted by both gods and mortals, it was probably not an apple as we know it, but a quince, another fruit native to the Middle East and brought back to Greece by the army.

HADES

One of three siblings (the other two being Zeus and Poseidon) who defeated their father Chronos and the gods known as Titans, to claim the cosmos for themselves. They proceeded to divide the cosmos up: Zeus got the skies, Poseidon the sea, and Hades, much to his annoyance, the Underworld. To everyone's confusion, the Underworld itself became known as Hades and the Romans renamed the god Hades, Pluto. They also renamed Zeus, Mickey Mouse, but it never really stuck.

HERACLES

A demi-god. The son of Zeus and Alcmene (a mortal), he possessed great strength, wit and courage. He is most famous for completing twelve labours as a penance for a terrible crime – murdering his wife and children after being driven temporarily insane by the jealous goddess Hera. He was a great adventurer and enjoyed playing games; one of his favourites was beating up lions.

HOPLITES

Soldiers who formed the backbone of the Greek army.

GARY'S GLOSSARY

They carried large, round shields and long spears. In battle, they would line up with their shields touching and their spears poking over the top in a formation known as a phalanx. Seeing a wall of shields and spears marching together in formation was enough to make anyone quake.

HESPERIDES

Goddess-nymphs entrusted to guard the golden apple tree. Gaia (the Goddess of Mother Earth) gave the tree to the goddess Hera as a wedding gift when she married Zeus. The nymphs and their glowing apples were celebrated as the source of the golden light of sunset.

KING MIDAS

An ancient king of Phrygia who, after helping the god Dionysus, asked that everything he touched would turn to gold. This was great until he tried to eat anything … or tried to hug his daughter! He begged for the gift to be taken back. Dionysus agreed, and Midas was instructed to wash his hands in the River Pactolus. Legend has it that that's why the sand in the river Pactolus is so golden to this day.

LABYRINTH

An elaborate and confusing maze. It was designed and built by the legendary architect Daedalus for King Minos of Crete in order to hold the Minotaur captive. Daedalus made the labyrinth so complex, he could barely escape it himself! And, when he finally did, Minos immediately imprisoned him and his son Icarus in order to preserve the labyrinth's secrets. But super-inventor Daedalus promptly made wings formed of feathers and wax and he and Icarus flew to freedom. Unfortunately, Icarus got a bit cocky and flew too close to the sun, his wax wings melted and … well, you can figure out the rest. There's a lesson in there somewhere!

LYRE

A stringed musical instrument played by the ancient Greeks. The god Apollo was considered a real virtuoso and he taught Orpheus to become the best of mortal musicians. Orpheus then used his lyre to sing his way into the Underworld on his journey to rescue his wife, Eurydice, from Hades.

GARY'S GLOSSARY

MINOTAUR

A monster with the head of a bull and the body of a man (or the head of a man, with the body of a bull, depending on who you listen to!). He was kept prisoner in the labyrinth by King Minos of Crete and regularly fed seven maidens and seven Athenian youths. Until, that is, the hero Theseus sneaked in and killed him. Theseus escaped the labyrinth by retracing his steps using string given to him by Minos's daughter, Ariadne. Quite simple when you think of it!

MOUNT OLYMPUS

Home to the pantheon of twelve Olympian gods (Zeus, Hera, Poseidon, Demeter, Athena, Hephaistus, Ares, Aphrodite, Apollo, Artemis, Hermes and Dionysus). High above the clouds and out of sight of mere mortals, here the gods ate, drank and argued like all normal families do, except the fate of the world lay in their hands. One god not invited up to Olympus was Hades, god of the Underworld. He'd say no if they asked him, anyway. Why would he want to sit on top of a stupid mountain, when he has an amazing vista of poisonous lakes and desolate fields filled with the roaming dead to look at?

NYMPHS

Nature goddesses. They ranked below the gods but were still summoned to attend assemblies on Mount Olympus. The nymphs controlled different aspects of nature – springs, clouds, trees, meadows and more – and cared for plants and animals. Different from other goddesses, nymphs are usually depicted as beautiful, young maidens who love to dance and sing.

ODYSSEY

One of the oldest and greatest stories in Western history, composed by the writer, Homer. It tells the story of Odysseus, King of Ithaca, and his ten year epic journey home from the Trojan Wars. He fought cyclops, six-headed monsters and even ghosts. In fact, it's placed only second in exciting Greek adventure stories after *Julius Zebra: Grapple with the Greeks!*

GARY'S GLOSSARY

OLYMPIC GAMES

Part of a religious celebration in honour of Zeus held in Olympia. At the first Games in 776 BC there was only one race, the stadion. This 600 foot long running race was won by Koroibos, a cook. According to some traditions, the stadion was the only race at the games for the first 13 festivals, before they decided it might be fun to do something else! The games are thought to have inspired the modern Olympic Games, begun in 1896.

RIVER STYX

The river that separated the world of the living from the world of the dead. The ancient Greeks believed its waters were deadly poisonous and would dissolve any container they were held in, except one made from the hoof of a horse or a donkey (or a zebra?).

TALOS

A bronze giant who guarded Crete. He was tasked with patrolling the island and circled it three times each day, throwing stones at the ships of unwanted visitors. His one weakness was his ankle, where a bronze nail was the only thing keeping his blood in place. That and going rusty in the rain, obviously.

TROJAN HORSE

A mightily suspicious giant wooden horse. After ten years of fighting in the Trojan War, the Greek army pretended to sail away from the city of Troy, leaving only the wooden horse behind. Never ones to refuse a present, the Trojans dragged the enormous horse inside the city. When night fell, some of the Greeks – who had been hiding in the hollow belly of the horse the entire time – jumped out, opened the city gates, and let the rest of the Greek army in to rampage through Troy.

ZEUS

King of the Olympian Gods. He sat on his throne atop Mount Olympus dispensing wisdom and punishments. He was also stronger than all of the gods put together and had the ability to throw lightning bolts and control the weather.

DRESS UP JULIUS AS AN

1. Photocopy, or trace around, the images on this page of Julius and the different parts of the Hoplite uniform.

2. Then glue the images onto thin sheets of card.

3. Cut around each of the shapes, as shown, and colour them in.

4. Now you can dress up Julius as an ancient Greek soldier by folding the small white tabs of the uniform carefully around his stripy body.

1.

2.

3.

Assemble Julius's stand like this!

ANCIENT GREEK HOPLITE!

Cut around black outlines.

Helmet

Shield

Linothorax

Spear

Pteruges

Greaves

Now what?

Bonus Herman the hermit crab!

BE IMMORTALIZED ON YOUR OWN GREEK JUG, OR URN!

1. Strike a dramatic pose.

2. Get a friend to draw you on a jug.

HOW TO PAINT IN THE ANCIENT GREEK STYLE

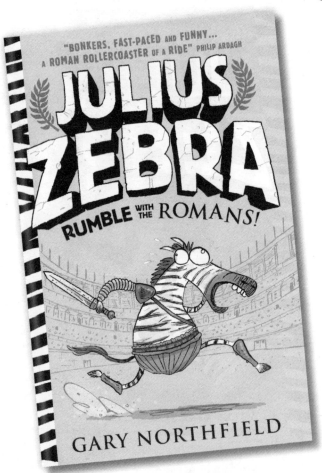

AND
**BUNDLING WITH THE
BRITONS!**

"A PLEASINGLY DAFT ROMP ... A VERY
HORRIBLE HISTORIES SENSE OF HUMOUR" FINANCIAL TIMES

**JULIUS
ZEBRA**

BUNDLE WITH THE
BRITONS!

GARY NORTHFIELD

BUT ... BEWARE OF GETTING
ENTANGLED WITH THE EGYPTIANS!

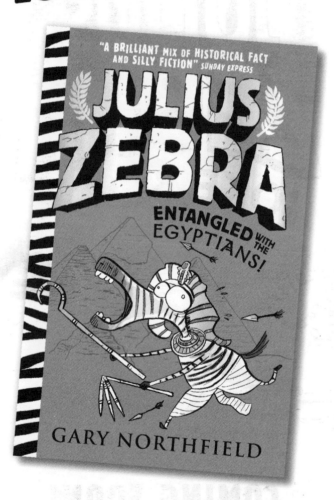

"A BRILLIANT MIX OF HISTORICAL FACT AND SILLY FICTION" SUNDAY EXPRESS

JULIUS ZEBRA

ENTANGLED WITH THE EGYPTIANS!

GARY NORTHFIELD

Gary Northfield is an award-winning
and bestselling author and illustrator of
children's books and comics. His bestselling
Julius Zebra series has now been translated
into ten languages worldwide and *Julius
Zebra: Rumble with the Romans!* won the
Spellbinding Book Award voted for by
children. Gary's other books include *The
Terrible Tales of the Teenytinysaurs!* (Walker)
and *Gary's Garden* (David Fickling) which
was nominated for the British Comic
Awards. Gary's work is also published
in *The Beano*, *The Dandy* and *National
Geographic Kids* among many other
magazines. He lives with his dog Stan,
partner Nicky and twins, Elsie and Arthur.
Together they have launched Bog Eyed
Books, a showcase for kids comics. Find
Gary online at www.garynorthfield.com,
on Twitter as @gnorthfield and Instagram
as @stupidmonster.